In Love, at War

By

Graysen Morgen

Triplicity Publishing

2013

In Love, at War © 2013 Graysen Morgen

Triplicity Publishing, LLC

ISBN-13: 978-0988619616

ISBN-10: 098861961X

Printed in the United States of America

First Edition – 2013

Cover Design: Triplicity Publishing, LLC

Interior Design: Triplicity Publishing, LLC

Also by Graysen Morgen

Falling Snow

Fate vs. Destiny

Just Me

Love, Loss, Revenge

Natural Instinct

Secluded Heart

Submerged

Acknowledgements

Special thanks to Lee Fitzsimmons, the person who spends countless hours correcting my mistakes. Also, a very special thanks to CJ and her Aussie eagle eyes.

Dedication

This book is dedicated to the brave men and women who gave their services during WWII. From the nurses, WASPs, and airmen to the sailors aboard the *USS Arizona* and *USS Oklahoma.*

Chapter One

Major Charlotte 'Charley' Hayes watched the sunrise in the most beautiful place she'd ever seen as she dressed in her drab, olive green colored utility uniform which was her daily work uniform. She was serving in the Women's Army Air Corps as the commanding officer for the Thirteenth Army Air Force Service Squadron, a fancy term for maintenance and airplane repair group. Her squadron was an all-female service squadron assigned to an Army Air Force Fighter Squadron stationed at NAS Ford Island which is how she wound up in Pearl Harbor. Basically, her job was leading a group of young women that repaired and serviced anything and everything mechanical in the Fighter Squadron they were assigned to.

She waited until the last minute to put the jacket on over her khaki colored t-shirt knowing the October Hawaiian sun was already beating down. She sipped the last of her black coffee, put her garrison cap on over her short, curly brown hair, and rushed out the door of Army Officer's Quarters, an old building that doubled as the barracks for her squadron.

She'd been there for close to four months and still wasn't used to the mixture of searing heat and cool ocean breeze. The dull squawk of seagulls flying overhead made her look up at the bright blue, cloudless sky and smile. Off in the distance she could see the mainland bustling with activity, and on the opposite side of the island Battleship Row was full of large dark-gray Navy ships casually anchored and bobbing up and down in the clear harbor water. The entire island felt as if there wasn't a care in the world.

Charley took her role as an Army Officer very seriously, demanding the same respect as any other officer male or female, but working at Pearl Harbor could loosen the tightest collar, and she'd learned to relax a bit and enjoy the beautiful scenery. The Fighter Squadron kept her squadron very busy, often times working on fighter plane repairs and handling maintenance schedules along with maintaining the unit's trucks and Jeeps.

She'd loved being a mechanic ever since she was a little girl when her dad had taught her about tools and the way machines worked. When she'd gotten a little older he began teaching her about planes. He'd taken her to the base with him on his days off to show her the planes he flew on and worked with everyday. She'd developed a love for planes and spent her teenage years working on the neighbor's old crop duster in exchange for laundry duties. The old man next door had been a widower and Charley would do his laundry for him and he would let her tinker with his plane. He tried to teach her how to fly it one year and she crashed it into the barn. After that she stayed on the ground. When she graduated from high school, Charley got a job working with her uncle at his small auto repair shop despite her mother's disapproval.

Charley's uncle taught her how to work on the cars and trucks he serviced daily and after a few months she had become one of his best mechanics. Over the next few years, in her spare time, Charley would work on other crop dusters and biplanes that were owned by friends of her neighbor. They had gladly accepted the free labor and allowed her to service their planes.

Charley had enjoyed working with her uncle, but she loved working on planes more and in 1940, the only place to have a career doing what she loved was in the military, so she'd joined and had gone through the four weeks of boot camp right away. When she had taken the aptitude test, the instructors were impressed by her answer choices and she had been permitted to go to Officer Candidate School. After twelve weeks of learning how to be an Army Air Force Officer, she had begun her mechanics training. When the Colonel of the mechanics school realized how much Charley already knew, she'd quickly been promoted up the ranks and by the end of the year she was commanding her own squadron of female mechanics. After only a few different posts, she'd been surprised when she was stationed at Ford Island in Pearl Harbor having been enlisted for just over a year.

"Good morning, Major," Sgt. Doris 'Higs' Higginbotham said as she hid a grin and saluted Charley. She was a little shorter than Charley with sandy colored, shoulder length hair pulled back in a tight bun.

"Higs." Charley saluted back and walked into the hangar. She shook her head when she looked around.

Their work area consisted of two massive hangars connected together that were big enough to house two large planes or four smaller fighters each. They were located on the edge of the runway so they also had a large staging area space outside to park planes and trucks waiting for service. Most of the time they were overloaded as the Service Squadron stationed at Hickam Field, which was the Army base across the harbor, decided to send them extra work that they didn't feel like doing. Charley often wondered if they did any work at all over there. Supposedly, that base was considered a 'hot zone' if they were to ever go to war and that's why the all-female unit was stationed on the Navy base. Apparently, the Navy base wasn't a threat to danger.

Charley wasn't surprised to see the three vehicles that had arrived earlier that morning before she was scheduled to be on shift. She went into the tiny closet she called an office and picked up the phone.

"Hickam Service Squadron. Maj. Parker speaking." The deep male voice answered.

"Parker, it's Hayes. What's with the two Jeeps and a utility truck that have mysteriously appeared here overnight?"

"We're backed up with plane repairs and those two needed their maintenance logs updated. I'm sure your *squadron* can handle it," he snickered.

Charley wanted to reach through the phone and claw his eyes out. "We're up to our eyeballs in plane repairs. I have two Kittyhawk pursuits sitting in pieces in one of my hangars and three Bolo bombers sitting outside awaiting parts. I don't have time to service *your* trucks. This better be the last damn time you do this," she spat and slammed the phone down.

"Higs," she yelled through the open door.

"Yes, ma'am." Higs rushed inside and stood at attention. As the only sergeant, she often found herself in charge of multiple tasks within the unit of fifteen women.

Charley relied on her to pull her weight and use her rank to her advantage. Most of the other women were corporals and a few were privates.

"Get those damn trucks out of my hair. Check their logs, it's probably oil changes or tire rotations or some stupid shit like that. We have two Peashooters and a Mohawk pursuit coming in this afternoon and we need the man power and parking space for them."

"Yes, ma'am." Higs saluted and pulled a group of three women together to knock the trucks out quickly and get back on the planes that were top priority.

Charley unbuttoned her utility jacket, hung it on the side of her tool box, and went to work installing the new parts on one of the Kittyhawk pursuits that was sitting in the hangar with its engine in pieces. She smiled when she heard the radio blaring close by. A radio was a hot commodity on the island and very hard to come by. Not long after the squadron first arrived, the women went in search of something to help the long hours go by when they had a shore pass. Higs had come back with a small short wave radio that picked up exactly two stations and cost her two weeks pay, but it had been worth it.

Chapter Two

The next day, Charley was hard at work on the same plane and excited that it was almost finished. She found herself dancing back and forth to her tool box as chart topping hits roared from the radio and bounced off the metal walls of the hangar. She could hear Higs singing along from her work area close by. She was glad to see the three trucks from the day before disappear, only to be replaced by three planes. It didn't matter how hard she worked, the workload seemed to constantly expand on top of her.

Charley was installing the headers to the engine and moved her hand slightly to adjust the light she had clipped to the side of the fuselage. The lighting in the hangar was severely lacking. When she moved her hand the header slipped. Jerking back to keep from squishing her hand, she smashed her forehead into the carburetor. Excruciating throbbing pain shot to her head and she was immediately dizzy as she fumbled her way down the ladder. She sat on the bottom step and pressed a rag to her forehead nonchalantly, hoping none of the other mechanics noticed the incident.

"You okay, Major? I saw that hawk bite you," Higs said from a few feet away.

"Yeah. I'm good," Charley murmured.

Higs walked closer and saw the blood seeping through the rag Charley was holding against her head. When Charley pulled it away to fold it into another section, Higs saw the inch wide gash above her eye.

"You need stitches. I'll drive you out to the hospital. The ferry should be running on time," she said, checking her watch.

"I'm fine. That landing gear's not going to fix itself while you stand here hemming and hawing over a little cut. Go back to work."

"Patterson, come take a look at the Major's head," Higs yelled across the hangar.

"Damn it, Higs. I'm fine."

Cpl. Elizabeth Patterson walked around the plane and grimaced when she saw the cut dripping blood. "I can see your brains. I think you better go to the hospital."

"Oh, good grief, Patterson. You do not see my brains. It's probably just meaty flesh and more than likely bone. Would you two please go back to work? We are still days behind as it is. I don't have time to go deal with the ferry and the hospital and all of that nonsense." Charley winced when she pressed the rag back to her head.

"Fine. At least let me take you to the dispensary. They can probably stitch it up." Higs put her hands on her hips and raised an eyebrow like a mother hen.

"The dispensary is a clinic. They give shots and see sick people," Charley argued.

"Major, they do the same things the hospital does, just at a lower level. Come on."

"Alright! But you're both working over time tonight because you're wasting time now," Charley growled as she stood up and walked outside to her assigned Jeep. The officers were the only personnel assigned vehicles on the island and nearby bases. The enlisted men and women usually bummed rides and shared cars when they could.

Thankfully, the drive over to the dispensary was short. Charley was holding on for dear life the entire time. Higs wasn't the best driver and she was driving as though Charley's head was hanging off her shoulders or something. There was no wait when they went inside and Charley was escorted to a gurney behind a crisp white curtain and told to wait for the nurse.

Charley was contemplating how she was going to get the blood out of her uniform when the curtain was pulled back and a beautiful woman stepped in. She was petite with long blond hair wrapped up in a tight bun behind her nurse's cap. She was wearing the khaki colored seersucker dress which was the Army Nurse Corps daily working uniform. The gold stripes on her uniform indicated she was a Chief Nurse. The Nurse Corps didn't have regular military ranks like the soldiers, sailors, and airmen.

The nurse noticed the blood on Charley's khaki t-shirt under her open green uniform jacket. She glanced at the gold leaf on the collar, indicating her rank and turned her smoky gray eyes up to meet Charley's green ones.

"I'm Nurse Sutton."

Charley suddenly felt light-headed and swayed on the gurney. The nurse quickly wrapped her arms around her to keep her from falling off. Charley's head pounded as she closed her eyes and inhaled the scent of fresh flowers wafting from the woman holding her.

"Major," the nurse said softly as she backed away enough to look at Charley's pupils.

"I'm fine," Charley said.

"Your pupils are dilated and you're dizzy. How exactly is that fine?" she said as she palpated the cut gently.

"I haven't eaten since breakfast. I must be hungry." Charley tried to calm the butterflies in her stomach before she embarrassed herself in front of the most beautiful woman she'd ever seen.

"Uh huh." The nurse wasn't buying it.

"I cut my head. It's really not a big deal and I wouldn't be here if two of my squad members hadn't driven me crazy instead of working."

"Well, Major Hayes, it looks like you need about six stitches, maybe eight," the nurse said.

"Wonderful," Charley huffed. "How long will it take?"

"Dr. Olsen is tied up with a sailor at the moment, but if you're in a hurry I can do it. I'm a Chief Nurse. I'll warn you though, it'll probably scar," the nurse said. She was nervous and her hands were slightly shaky. The last thing she wanted to do was leave a scar on the stunningly handsome face looking back at her.

"I don't care, just sew it up. I have planes on top of planes waiting for repairs and I'm wasting time sitting here."

The nurse had Charley lay back and she prepped her head, cleaning the wound with iodine before sewing the cut closed with seven bright blue stitches. During the short procedure, she questioned Charley about where she was stationed and what her duties were. When she finished she gave her a handout with information on caring for a concussion. Charley thanked her and tossed the pamphlet in the trash on the way out.

Charley's entire squadron razzed her about the stitches when she returned to the hangar until she remade the schedule for the next week and a half giving everyone fourteen hour shifts to try and get ahead of their workload.

Finally arriving back at the barracks for the night, Charley's head was hurting so badly she could hardly drive herself, but she wasn't about to let Higs drive her anywhere ever again. She was thankful they all had separate rooms and were only two to a bathroom. They were the only all-female squad on the island and had the building to themselves. She took a quick shower and went straight to bed, willing the throbbing to go away. She had to be up earlier than usual because they had two planes with new engines installed and were scheduled for test flights after the sun came up. She needed to be there for those flights and wasn't entirely happy that the flight squadron commander scheduled them so early to begin with. Then again, she was used to getting screwed over by her male counterparts on a daily basis.

Chapter Three

It had been close to two weeks since Charley had cut her head and she was now happily back to normal and surprised to be ahead of schedule for a change. Thanksgiving was fast approaching and she knew her squad was going to want liberty to celebrate on the mainland. She had her head buried in the engine compartment of a Bolo trying to get the fuel line reconnected. The plane was already on the test flight schedule and she was rushing to make the two hour deadline.

"Patterson, hand me that socket wrench," Charley said without looking down. When she felt the cool wrench touch her hand she said, "Thanks."

"You're welcome," a soft voice answered in return.

Charley's head popped up and she smacked the back of it on the compartment hatch. She turned around to see the beautiful, smiling woman wearing an Army Nurse Corps Dress Uniform, gazing up at her.

"Nurse Sutton," Charley said nonchalantly as she rubbed the back of her head and climbed down the ladder.

"It looks like you bump your head a lot, Major," she said shyly.

Charley wiped her hands on the rag she pulled from her back pocket. "I'm afraid it appears that way. What can I do for you?"

The nurse took in her attire. Charley wasn't wearing her utility jacket; instead she was wearing a sweat-soaked khaki undershirt with grease stains in odd places. Her hair was clinging to her forehead and the back of her neck in small ringlets.

She quickly straightened her posture and cleared her throat. "I noticed you hadn't come back to have your stitches taken out and I was in the area so I thought I'd stop by."

"I took them out myself," Charley said.

"I see that." She smiled. "Well, I should probably go then."

"Excuse me, nurse?" Higs said from the other side of the plane. When Audrey turned around Higs walked over to her. "What's your first name?"

"Audrey."

"Audrey, would you like to celebrate Thanksgiving with a bunch of mechanics tomorrow night?" Higs put on her best smile.

Audrey turned back towards Charley.

'Thanks, but I probably shouldn't. I'm on shift Friday."

"So are we." Higs grinned.

"We've had enough turkey this week in the mess hall so I gave them liberty for the evening. We're going to the mainland to some Thanksgiving Social," Charley said.

Audrey smiled realizing the Major was going too and turned to Higs. "I'd love to go."

Charley and Higs watched her walk away with her khaki shirt blowing in the breeze.

"Does she have any nurse friends?"

Charley looked at Higs and shrugged before walking back to the bomber she was working on. She had received a call that morning saying two trucks were coming in from Ewa. It was an Army and Marine Corps air field a little further away than Hickam on the mainland. She wasn't exactly pleased, but she was tired of arguing with the arrogant men. The trucks would have to wait. The Havoc bombers, Mohawk, and Kittyhawk pursuits sitting on the tarmac in front of the hangars, were first in line and awaiting various repairs or maintenance updates.

***

Charley stared at herself in the mirror. She was wearing her WAAC Dress Uniform which was a khaki shirt and pants with a khaki tie and an olive green jacket with gold buttons. She was proud of the gold leaf on the collar. She'd worked hard to become a Major and her greatest accomplishment was being able to command her own squadron. She checked the shine on her black loafers one last time, put her garrison cap on her head, and walked out of her room.

"You clean up nice, Major." Higs joked and smacked her on the shoulder. She and Patterson were also wearing their WAAC Dress Uniforms, but they weren't as shiny and spiffy as Charley's because they weren't officers.

"I'd say the same for you Higs, but your shoes are barely polished and your pants are wrinkled," Charley teased.

"We better get going if we're going to make the ferry on time." Patterson pushed them both towards the front door of the building.

When they arrived at the nurse's barracks on the other side of the island, Audrey was waiting with two other women. They were all wearing summer dresses with their hair hanging down. Charley was slightly jealous of the nurses when she saw their attire, although she wasn't a dress wearer herself. The Nurse Corps were the only personnel allowed out of uniform. All of the airmen and sailors were required to be in uniform at all times whether they were on the island or not.

Charley, Higs and Patterson got out of the Jeep, walking up to the waiting women.

"Good evening, Major. I hope you don't mind, but a few of my friends wanted to join us," Audrey said.

"No, not at all and please call me Charley. This is Higs, whom you've met, and Patterson."

"It's nice to meet you," Audrey smiled, shaking their hands. "This is Sharon," she said pointing to the slender woman with poufy red hair. "And this is Francine."

Francine brushed her dark hair off her shoulder, saying, "Please, call me Fran."

"It's going to be a tight fit, but I think we can manage," Audrey said as they climbed into the Jeep. Since it was an old, customary open top Army Jeep with a manual transmission, there were only two seats up front. Charley climbed in and sat behind the wheel and Audrey claimed shotgun. The other four women had to squish together in the back. All of the nurses held their hair to keep from being windblown as they drove across the island.

They crossed to the harbor, parked the Jeep close to the ferry landing, and walked through the small town. Most of the bars and restaurants were participating in the holiday dance. They stopped when they came upon a restaurant with a bar and a dance floor that was already hopping with airmen and sailors.

"This place looks good." Higs led the way and found a corner table big enough for everyone.

"Have you ever been here?" Audrey looked at Charley.

Charley shook her head no and opened her menu. The waiter appeared and Charley ordered two fried seafood platters for the table and a whiskey and water for herself.

Halfway through their meal, the women were laughing and talking about life in Hawaii when a guy in a uniform that closely resembled Charley's appeared next to their table.

"Major Hayes, it's nice to see you get off the island once in a while."

Charley plastered a fake smile on her face.

"I couldn't resist coming to the mainland to celebrate giving thanks. So, thanks, Major Parker," she said sarcastically. Higs and Patterson laughed hysterically when he walked away with an odd look on his face.

"He's such a dickless prick." Higs took a swig from her beer mug.

Charley shook her head and toasted her in agreement.

"Who was that?" Audrey asked.

"A huge pain in the ass," Higs answered.

"He's the CO for the service squadron at Hickam Field," Charley said.

"He's the one that sends us maintenance jobs that his squad is too lazy to do, causing us to work fourteen hour days," Patterson added.

"We came to have fun. Let's dance." Sharon got up from the table and wiggled out to the middle of the dance floor. The rest of the group slowly followed. They joined the other jitterbugs on the floor who were already dancing the Lindy Hop swing dance to music by the Andrews Sisters.

Charley hadn't really let her hair down much since she'd donned her uniform for the first time and she was surprised at how much she was enjoying the evening. She found herself dancing close to Audrey during many of the fast songs. When the slower songs came on, all of the women left the dance floor using that as an excuse to have another drink.

Charley wiped the sweat from her brow with her napkin and finished her watered down glass of whiskey.

"You're a good dancer, Major." Audrey sat down in the seat next to her, dabbing her face with her napkin, careful not to smear her light make-up.

"Thanks."

"You should see her in the hangar. She Lindy Hops back and forth from her toolbox to wherever she's working. That's how we know she's in a good mood. If the Major isn't dancing, we're in for a long day." Patterson grinned.

Audrey laughed and followed the rest of the women back to the dance floor for another Andrews Sisters song. A half hour later, Audrey noticed Charley was missing. She walked around the inside of the restaurant bar then decided to look outside. She found her leaning on the rail a few feet away looking out at Battleship Row.

"It's quiet out here."

Charley turned her head when she heard the soft voice.

"I needed some air," Charley said.

Audrey walked up next to her and studied her face in the moonlight.

"Your cut healed better than I thought it would. I'm sorry you have a scar."

"It gives me character." Charley smiled.

Audrey reached up and silently ran her finger over the raised line above Charley's eye. Charley backed away, gasping at the sudden contact.

Audrey hung her head and turned to walk away. Charley grabbed her hand and pulled the petite woman against her. Audrey's light gray eyes were dark and smoky in the low light. Charley bent her head slightly, softly pressing her lips to Audrey's. Audrey ran her hands up the front of Charley's uniform and into the hair at the back of her neck as she parted her lips to allow the kiss to deepen. Charley ran her tongue around the edge of Audrey's lips before going inside and claiming what Audrey was offering.

Charley felt Audrey's hips move against hers, bringing her back to reality. They were standing out in the open and could easily be seen. She quickly pulled away and adjusted her cap and uniform jacket.

"I'm sorry," she said.

"Don't be. I wanted that as much as you did, maybe more," Audrey said.

Charley looked at her and grinned. She couldn't believe this beautiful woman was coming onto her. It was 1941 and there weren't many 'sisters' out and about.

"Do you want to get out of here?" Charley asked.

"Yes," Audrey whispered.

Charley went inside and told everyone that Audrey wasn't feeling well and she was going to drive her back. The rest of them would have to take a base taxi when they got back to the island, but she didn't care. It had been a few years since she'd been with another woman. She was beyond nervous and extremely excited.

Charley drove to her barracks building praying most of the other women were still out for the night. She parked the Jeep in the front and led Audrey inside and up the stairs to her small room. There was a tiny desk on one side with a matching wooden chair and a foot locker next to it along with a long mirror on the wall next to the closet. The other side of the room had an old single bed up against the wall with the Army issued sheets and scratchy wool blanket tucked in perfectly and a rickety night stand next to it.

Charley shut the door, walked passed Audrey, and lit the oil lamp on the nightstand. When she returned to the doorway, Audrey slowly unbuttoned Charley's jacket one gold button at a time. She pushed it off her shoulders, draped it over the desk chair, and went to work loosening her tie and opening the buttons on her shirt. Charley kicked her shoes off and untied the tie at the top of the back of Audrey's dress. She slid the dress off her shoulders and watched it pool around her feet at the floor. Audrey loosened Charley's belt, opened her pants, and pushed them down her legs.

Both women stopped and stared at each other. Audrey was wearing a camisole and matching panties and Charley was wearing a white undershirt and what looked like Army issued underwear.

"We can stop..."

Audrey pressed her fingers to Charley's lips. Charley opened her mouth, sucking the fingers gently. Audrey swallowed the lump in her throat and felt her pulse rising. Charley wrapped her arms around Audrey and walked her the few short steps to the bed. Audrey pulled her fingers away and lay back on the bed. Charley crawled on top of her and kissed her way from the top of the open camisole to her soft skin below her ear and up to her lips. Audrey's hips rose up against her and Charley slid her tongue inside her mouth over and over with each movement of Audrey's hips. Both women pulled away from the kiss, panting and began stripping off the rest of the clothing separating them.

Charley laid down on Audrey once again and pressed their naked bodies together. Audrey's heart was beating so fast she thought she might pass out when she felt the softness of Charley's skin against hers. Her hips moved on their own accord as Charley ran her hand over Audrey's body from her legs to her stomach. She placed soft kisses on each breast before squeezing it and sucking the nipple into her mouth.

"Oh god!" Audrey cried out. Charley quickly put her mouth on Audrey's to silence her. If any of the other women were in the barracks, they would hear Audrey and both women would be kicked out of the service and who knows what else.

Charley smiled when she pulled away slightly.

"Sorry," Audrey whispered shyly.

Charley rolled over, pulling Audrey on top of her. She ran her hands over her back under the soft waves of her hair and down to her butt, softly squeezing and pulling Audrey tightly against her as she slipped her thigh between Audrey's legs. Audrey's wetness coated her leg

24

as Charley moved her back and forth against her. She watched the changes in Audrey's face as her body began opening up like a flower in the sunshine. Charley moved her back over and ran her hand down her side to the wetness between her legs. Audrey gasped and held her breath as Charley moved her fingers through the silky folds in lazy circles. Hers hips jerked and rose with every pass over her clit. Audrey began clinching the bed sheets and moving frantically under Charley as she pushed two fingers inside her and was surprised at how tight her opening was. Audrey winced and moaned and Charley quickly backed away and pulled her fingers out.

"Please don't stop," Audrey whispered breathlessly.

Charley pushed her fingers back inside and began moving them in and out slowly. Audrey opened a little more with every thrust until Charley was easily moving deeper inside and almost all the way out of her. The rickety bed under them began creaking with every thrust but neither woman noticed.

Audrey panted, gasping for air between moans. Her hips pushed down on Charley's hand every time her fingers moved deep inside of her. Charley held her and kissed her tenderly when she felt Audrey spasm around her fingers.

"Oh god...oh!" Audrey cried out as the orgasm washed over her with smaller waves coming behind it over and over. Charley held her as Audrey's body jerked and shivered until it was over.

"Oh my," Audrey whispered when she finally caught her breath.

Charley kissed her, letting her tongue linger inside before pulling away and sliding down her body. The patch of light colored hair was glistening in the soft glow of the lamp. Charley spread Audrey's legs, sliding her tongue over the shimmering pink folds. Audrey bucked and gasped. Charley grabbed the bed sheet to keep from being tossed to the floor. She smiled and moved more of her weight to Audrey's legs as she licked her again, applying more pressure this time.

Audrey bit her bottom lip to keep from screaming as Charley licked and sucked her over and over. Every time Charley's tongue passed her entrance, she pushed it inside then back out again. Audrey thought she was going to literally fly apart into thousands of pieces and die right here. She reached down, ran her hand through Charley's curls, and pressed her hips against her mouth. Charley took the sign and sucked harder.

Audrey snatched the pillow out from under her head, put it over her face, and screamed into it as her body began quivering. Charley held her down, licking and sucking until she felt warm liquid coat her tongue. She licked her way back up Audrey's body, laughing when she pulled the pillow off her face. Audrey's eyes were as black as the night sky.

"I didn't know you could do that," she whispered. She was still trying to catch her breath.

"No one's ever done that?" Charley said as she moved next to her and pushed the hair from Audrey's sweat-soaked forehead.

"No. I've never..." Audrey turned her head.

Charley sat up. "Never? Never what?"

"I've never done any of that."

"What!? You mean you haven't...not with anyone?"

"No."

Charley ran her hand through her hair.

"It's okay, Charley. I wanted to do it."

"Why me?"

"I knew the first time I saw you that something was different. I had this feeling inside. That's why I went to see you at the hangar. I had to see you again. I can't explain it."

"Audrey, you don't want this life. Living in secret, scared someone will find out. It's wrong."

"I don't care about anyone else. It's not wrong to be with someone that makes you feel the way you make me feel, Charley."

"This could ruin our careers if someone finds out."

"I don't care. I love being a nurse, but the Army isn't my life."

"How old are you?" Charley asked.

"Twenty-two. You?"

Charley cleared her throat. "Closer to thirty," she said.

Charley wondered if she was making a huge mistake. All she'd ever wanted to do was serve in the Army like her father had done before he died in combat during WWI. If she was caught being a 'sister' it would be the end of everything she had worked so hard to get.

Audrey pulled Charley down for another searing kiss causing the thoughts in her head to fade away. Audrey ended the kiss and pushed Charley to her back.

"Show me how to touch you."

"Some women don't..."

"I want to touch you, but I don't know how. Show me, Charley. Please?" Audrey said.

Charley grabbed Audrey's hand, running it over her body, stopping to let her feel her breasts one at a time. Then, she spread her legs and moved Audrey's hand lower, sliding her fingers through the wetness between them. She swirled Audrey's fingers around her clit in large circles, then closing into smaller circles before she pushed her fingers inside.

Audrey was on her own at that point and began moving her fingers in and out, mimicking what Charley had done to her. She was surprised at how warm and wet it felt to be inside of another woman. She loved the way the muscles tightened around her every time she pushed her fingers deeper.

Charley gripped the sheets with one hand and ran the other hand over Audrey's back and into the hair fanning out across it. She bit back a moan, pushing her hips down to meet every thrust until her body tightened. She held Audrey against her and rode the waves of pleasure.

Audrey pulled her fingers out gently and made lazy strokes as she painted a path back up to Charley's breasts. She kissed Charley's lips softly, making her chase for a deeper kiss.

"Can I do that again?" Audrey asked when the kiss broke.

Charley laughed quietly. "I think I may have woken a sleeping dragon."

"Oh really?" Audrey raised an eyebrow and grinned as her fingers slid back down Charley's body.

Charley jerked and grabbed her hand before it landed on her throbbing center.

"Give me a minute to catch my breath," she said, bringing Audrey's hand to her mouth to kiss her own wetness from her fingers.

Chapter Four

It had been close to one a.m. when she'd finally taken Audrey back to her barracks and Charley's tiredness showed in her baggy eyes and the four cups of coffee she drank this morning. She still had a full ten hour day ahead of her if she wanted to stay caught up and get those planes in the air for test-runs before dark. Her mind kept drifting back to Audrey lying naked in her bed, causing her to dropped more tools than she could count.

"You okay, Major?" Patterson asked after she heard the wrench hit the floor and Charley swear for the fifth time.

"Yeah, I'm fine. I didn't get enough sleep last night, I guess," she said nonchalantly, picking up the wrench and going back to working on the wing she was repairing.

Charley was lost in thought when she heard shouting in the distance over the music from the radio. She rolled her eyes and finished the last line of rivets on the wing of the Peashooter she had been working on all day. One of the arrogant hot shot pilots couldn't judge distance and had smashed into another plane on the tarmac causing both to need repairs.

"You better get these women in line, Hayes," a loud male voice echoed in the hangar.

Charley raised an eyebrow, swung her legs around, and slid down the wing, landing softly a few feet from the shouting airman.

"Excuse me? What was that?" she said, wiping her hands on the rag she pulled from her back pocket.

"You heard me. You women have no fucking clue what you're doing and you're wasting my time."

Charley tossed the rag on the ground, moving within an inch of the guy as she looked at the collar of his flight suit. Her lips formed a thin straight line.

"First of all, I suggest you address me as Major or ma'am. I do believe I am your superior officer, Lieutenant. Secondly, you owe me and my squadron an apology. Thirdly, if you don't get out of my hangar I'm going to throw you out on your ass, you little weasel."

"You can't..." he stumbled backwards. "I'm going to the CO."

"Good, you do that. While you're at it, tell him you're over here causing a huge distraction which has only led to my staff getting behind because we've had to stop and baby-sit pansy-assed pilots like yourself. Now, if you'd like to actually do your job, I have a Peashooter that's ready for a test flight."

"Fine, ma'am." He rolled his eyes and turned away.

"Lieutenant, I suggest you stand at attention when you address me."

Carl Davis rolled his eyes, but straightened up.

"Yes, ma'am."

"That's better. Now, go apologize to whoever you were screaming at and I'll roll this plane out. Be ready in five."

Charley watched him walk to the other hangar before calling Patterson and one of the other corporals, a young girl named Shirley Lowe, over to help her roll the plane out onto the tarmac.

"He's such a jerk every time he comes over here," Patterson said. "I thought you were going to punch him out. Personally, I would've cheered you on."

Charley laughed. "What does Higs call him? Dickless? He's just a hot-shot, young pilot with a little too much excitement. He probably hasn't been in the Army Air Force long enough to get his panties wet. I'm sure he's pissed he was assigned to fly the test flights, but flying is flying and stationed on this island away from everything he should be excited to fly a paper plane. Besides, with all of the idiot damage we've been fixing lately, I'm not sure any of those turkeys even know how to fly a plane."

Charley climbed inside the Peashooter and pushed the choke while Patterson spun the props. Lt. Davis finally appeared when the plane was warmed up and ready to go. She climbed out and returned his salute before going back to the hangar. She didn't wait around to see the plane fly; she had two more just like it awaiting routine maintenance checks and the day was quickly disappearing on her.

"Is that Davis?" Higs said, standing outside of the hangar, readying another plane for its test flight.

"Yeah."

"I'd love to smack his teeth out," Higs said.

"Wouldn't we all? Is this the Mohawk you put the new landing gear on?"

"Yes, and the next one of the damn rookie pilots who breaks a landing gear can come install the new one himself." Higs wiped the grease from her hands and pushed the rag back into her pocket.

"I'm assuming Davis is assigned to us today since he has his knickers in a twist. Call over and have them send him back to fly this cat before we lose the last of the light. He's wasted enough of our time already. If his CO gives you a problem, let me know." Charley walked inside the hangar, going back to work checking the Scout waiting for her attention.

***

Two days later, Charley was ready to call it a night when Higs and Patterson cornered her.

"Major, did you see there's a new picture show playing on the mainland?" Patterson asked.

"No."

"Everyone's talking about it. We should all go," Higs grinned widely.

"Let me get this straight. You two want to go see it and since I have wheels you thought you'd talk me into going too. Is that correct?" Charley began walking towards the barracks.

"Come on, Major. Maybe we can get those nurses to go with us," Patterson pleaded.

Charley stopped walking and turned around, glaring green daggers at Higs. She'd regretted outing herself to Higs and surely she and Patterson had discussed her impromptu visits with Nurse Sutton. She wondered how much longer her career was going to stay afloat with Twiddle Dee and Twiddle Dumb and their big mouths.

"Go get changed. I'm leaving in ten minutes," Charley huffed. Both women leaned over and kissed her cheeks.

"You're the greatest CO ever," Patterson squealed.

Charley turned around to see if anyone had noticed the childish display of affection.

"See, I told you she'd go if we mentioned the nurse." Charley heard Higs say on her way down the hall.

True to her word, ten minutes later Charley was backing the Jeep out of the parking space when Higs and Patterson came running out of the building. She barely gave them time to jump in before driving off towards the nurse barracks on the other side of the island. The moon was full and high, casting a light blue glow on the ships docked at Battleship Row as they drove by.

The Jeep skidded to a halt in front of the large white building behind the dispensary. Higs moved to get out of the Jeep, but stopped when Charley grabbed her wrist.

"I'll go. Who knows if they have some kind of curfew or something and it's best if there is an officer calling on them at this hour."

Charley walked up the steps and knocked on the door. She removed her garrison cap when a grey-haired woman dressed in a nurse's uniform opened the door and waved her inside.

"I'm here to see Audrey Sutton." Charley stood at attention, proudly displaying her WAAC Dress Uniform.

"May I ask what your business is with Nurse Sutton, at this hour," The woman asked.

"I need to ask her a question about a prescription she gave me this afternoon," Charley lied.

"What's the prescription? I can help you with that."

Charley swallowed the lump in her throat. "I uh...I don't have it with me. I'm sorry. I thought she might remember. See it's for this itch..."

"I will get her. Please wait right here, Major," the woman said as she took off up the stairs. Charley laughed quietly.

The groan from the worn staircase brought Charley's attention to the beautiful woman bouncing down the stairs towards her. Audrey's blond hair was flowing in loose waves behind her with a light blue ribbon tied in the front to keep it out of her face. She was wearing a thin summer dress that matched the ribbon. Charley smiled, but quickly hid her eyes from the older woman making her way slowly down the stairs.

"Major Hayes, what can I do for you?" Audrey grinned.

"We're going to see a picture show and I wanted to see if you could get away and go with us, but the warden there thinks I have an itch that you gave me a prescription for and I have questions about it."

Audrey laughed and turned around to face the Head Nurse as she came down the last couple of steps.

"Head Nurse Klein, I need to go check out the Major's barracks. It seems a few more people have the uh...the itch...too. I should probably take Fran with me."

"Is it that bad? Maybe they should wait until morning and go to the dispensary."

Audrey grimaced. "They probably shouldn't wait that long."

Charley began shuffling back and forth on her feet and moving inconspicuously as if she were trying not to scratch an itch in a private area. The Head Nurse's eyebrows rose into her hairline and she stepped back.

"Fine. Go get Nurse Dobbs and take Nurse Keiser too. Good luck with that uh...itch, Major," she said as she went back to her room next to the staircase.

"I'll meet you outside," Audrey said quietly and hurried back up the stairs.

Charley slid into the driver's seat of the Jeep and started the engine.

"You two clowns owe me big," Charley growled.

Higs and Patterson high-fived each other when they saw all three women come out of the building.

"How's that itch, Major?" Fran said when she got in the Jeep.

Charley floored the gas and drove away without answering. The Jeep bounced along the uneven road and came to a stop next to the ferry landing.

"So what are we going to see?" Audrey asked.

Charley shrugged.

"Suspicion," Higs said.

Charley turned around and glared at Higs.

"I'm serious. It's the new Hitchcock picture," Higs grinned.

"Is it scary?" Audrey asked.

"Yeah, but we're with the Major and she's not scared of anything. You'll be fine," Patterson said.

Charley rolled her eyes and shook her head. This was the last time she was letting them drag her off the island. When the ferry docked, they drove through the small town and parked on the side street, a block away from the cinema.

Each woman paid twenty-five cents for her own ticket at the box office. They also bought sodas and a couple tubs of popcorn before going to their seats.

Cary Grant and Joan Fontaine starred in the black and white thriller about man who courts a woman he just met, marries her right away, then she suspects he is trying to kill her for the insurance money. During one particularly intense moment, all of the women in the room gasped and screamed. Audrey put her hand on top of Charley's and squeezed. Charley smiled and held her hand through the rest of the picture.

When they walked back to the Jeep, Higs was still reeling from excitement. "I thought for sure he was going to toss her out of the car!"

"Oh, me too!" Fran squeaked.

"I don't think he was good enough for her. I was hoping she would kill him," Patterson added. Everyone turned to look at her. "What?" she said.

Charley laughed. "I think I will drive us back at break-neck speed and see if anyone falls out."

"No you will not," Audrey waved a finger at her.

Charley grinned and stopped walking when they reached the malt shop in the strip where they parked the Jeep. Everyone followed her inside and gathered around the small corner table. Charley ordered a chocolate malt and waited while the other women ordered various flavors. She couldn't remember the last time she'd had so much fun, well except for the night Audrey spent with her not long ago. She wasn't ready to return to their base, but it was uncustomary for women to be out late and it was already past late.

When the Jeep finally rolled back onto the island from the ferry, Charley floored the gas and see-sawed the wheel as the small open vehicle lurched back from side to side. Everyone was holding on for dear life as they raced around the island. She raised an eyebrow when she looked in the side mirror and noticed Fran was in Higs' arms to keep from falling out.

"Charley!" Audrey screamed.

Charley laughed and slowed down as she came up on the dispensary building and the nurses' barracks.

"That was not nice," Audrey said. "You scared me to death." The color was slowly coming back to her face.

"I'm sorry." Charley reached over and squeezed her hand when what she really wanted to do was pull the beautiful woman into her arms and kiss her soft lips.

"Thanks for asking us to go," Fran said, climbing out behind Audrey.

"I think you really pissed her off," Higs said, climbing into the front seat. They waited for the nurses to get safely inside before driving off.

Chapter Five

The next day, Charley was doing routine maintenance checks on a B-17 Flying Fortress bomber and singing along to *Chattanooga Choo Choo* on the radio. She wasn't happy about having to work the upcoming weekend. They were behind schedule thanks again to Hickam sending them a half a dozen planes that needed maintenance checks, on top of the few planes and couple of trucks that were being repaired.

Charley climbed down the ladder to get a wrench to tighten the loose oil line she'd found in her inspection. She was searching her toolbox when she heard the soft click of heels on the hangar floor. Charley turned around and smiled.

"You have some grease..."

Audrey walked over and ran her finger across Charley's cheek. Charley wiped her face with a clean rag.

"What brings you out here? I wasn't sure if I would see you again."

Audrey smiled. "It's a beautiful day and I was thinking of having a picnic lunch. I'm still mad at you by the way, but can you get away?"

Charley looked around the double hangar. Half of her squadron was working and the other half was at the mess hall eating lunch. She shrugged.

"Let me see if Higs is back from lunch." Charley walked away.

Audrey looked at the four planes sitting side-by-side across the hangar with two trucks parked inside on the end. A radio was blaring in the distance and it smelled like grease and gas. She was careful not to touch anything or step in any of the puddles on the floor.

"I have a half hour," Charley said when she returned.

Audrey walked outside to the coupe parked next to the hangar.

"Where did you get this?" Charley asked.

"I borrowed it from Dr. Olsen. I think he has a crush on me."

Charley laughed, "Oh really?"

"Yes. Come on, we don't have a lot of time."

"I'll follow you." Charley walked over to her Jeep and the coupe sped away. She started it quickly and wound through the gears as she drove across the island. Both of the vehicles came to a stop at a small beach area with picnic tables on the opposite side of Battleship Row. They were facing the East Loch and had an unobstructed view since they were away from the ships.

Audrey spread a blanket in the sand and sat down with a light brown colored wicker basket. Charley sat next to her and stretched her legs out.

"I'm sorry I scared you last night."

"It's okay. I was glad I got to see you."

"I've been so busy I barely have time to sleep. I swear I think the CO at Hickam thinks we're joining this war soon. He has sent me just about every plane and truck from his fleet in the last two weeks. I'd like to know what the Service Squadron over there is doing, because it's definitely not fixing planes and trucks, that's for sure. I know the Flight Squadron has been practicing a lot of drills. Ours has too."

"Do you think we'll be in the war soon?" Audrey squeezed her hand and passed her a chicken salad sandwich.

Charley shrugged and took a bite, still holding Audrey's in hers. She grinned when her stomach growled.

"I don't know. I mean war is imminent, it's just a matter of when and how we will enter it, I guess. Personally, I think we should just let everyone else handle their own battles and keep our noses out of it. I'll be glad when it's over. I was happy when we first got to Pearl. Our workload was light and life was laidback. Now, our workload has tripled in the last three weeks and we barely have time to eat lunch or see the people we care about."

"You care about me?" Audrey smiled.

"Maybe," Charley finished her sandwich and peeked in the basket.

"I don't think trying to toss me out of a vehicle is a good way to show you care about someone," Audrey chided.

Charley sighed. "I said I was sorry. I didn't realize that picture scared you so bad."

"It didn't really scare me, but you did when you started driving like a maniac. I realized later that it was all fun and games and you guys take the fun where you can get it. I understand."

"I shouldn't have done it anyway. I'm an officer and that was conduct unbecoming for sure. If someone had seen me you might be reading a letter right now instead of sitting here with me."

"You're too careful to get caught doing anything. When you do actually do something, it's a little too far left."

"Like caring for you when I shouldn't." Charley whispered, reaching for whatever else was in the basket.

"Maybe, but I think it's Higs you care about. You sure spend a lot of time together," Audrey teased and closed the basket on her hand.

"Higs?" Charley laughed. "She's not a 'sister'."

"Really? I could've sworn Fran said she..."

"No. I doubt it," Charley lay back with her hands under her head and looked up at the sun.

"I miss you," Audrey said.

"I miss you too."

"Do you get liberty this weekend?"

"No. We're working the next ten days straight. I might be able to sneak away Sunday afternoon. We're only scheduled for half a day since we have to allow time for church services."

"It's a date then," Audrey said.

Charley tried so hard to fight off the growing attraction to Audrey. She knew the nurse was young and had only had Charley as a partner. She wondered when the other shoe would drop and break her heart or when they'd get caught and be made into fools. At the same time, she wanted nothing more than to spend every night making love to the beautiful woman, no matter what the consequences were.

"I should probably get back. I told Higs I had to drive out to Wheeler to get some parts." Charley sat up.

Audrey laughed.

"What are you going to say when you come back without the parts?"

"Those bozos never have anything right over there. I'll just tell her they couldn't find the parts."

"Why didn't you tell her you were going to lunch?"

"I don't take a lunch. Usually, someone brings me something from the mess hall. Lately, I eat when I find the time."

"Are you worried someone will find out about us?"

"Always. Aren't you?"

"I don't know. This is all so new for me. I guess I haven't experienced the cruel side of being a 'sister'."

"Hopefully, you never do, Audrey." Charley leaned over and kissed her lips softly.

"Promise I'll see you Sunday?" Audrey said.

"Cross my heart." Charley smiled and double-timed it back to the Jeep. She was already running late and no doubt Higs would have questions that she didn't have answers to.

***

The sun wasn't even up yet when Higs climbed into the Jeep with Charley. The rest of the girls on the squadron had caught the small bus that shuttled sailors and aircrew around the island.

"How did you miss the bus?" Charley asked.

"Shirley was hogging the bathroom and I was running late. The bigger question is why are you running late since you're the one that scheduled us to be at the hangar at 0730 on Sunday morning?"

42

"I was up late last night," Charley parked on the opposite side of where she normally parked since there was a truck sitting in her usual spot.

"Uh huh, so has Audrey said anything about Fran?"

"What?" Charley got out and turned around to look at her.

"Oh come on, I know you and Audrey..."

"What about me and Nurse Sutton?" Charley stood at attention.

"Calm down." Higs stepped closer. "I'm a 'sister' too and so is Patterson."

"Sister?" Charley raised an eyebrow as if she didn't understand.

Higs cleared her throat and rolled her eyes. "Sisters, as in we...you know."

"No shit!?" Charley said a little too loudly.

"No shit. So...has Fran said anything about me?"

"I have no idea and how many people know you're...that we're...'sisters'?"

"Just me and Patterson. We kind of assumed you were, but after the way Audrey looked at you the first time and keeps coming around, it's pretty clear."

Charley took her cap off and twisted it before putting it back on. "Keep this between us, okay, Higs? If anyone found out..."

"I know. I know. Trust me. I don't care to suffer the consequences either."

"Let's go. We have work to do."

"Can you put in a good word to Fran for me?"

Charley huffed and shook her head. "I'm not getting involved."

"Come on, Major. Just ask Audrey if Fran likes me."

"I'll see what..." Charley was cut off by the loud buzzing of low flying planes. She walked out a few feet away from the hangar and looked up at the sky. A large group of planes was flying in a V formation towards them and low enough that the bombs could be seen in the racks and the pilots in the cockpits. Charley was confused. The planes looked like Kates, which were Japanese bombers.

As the planes passed overhead, Charley tried to read the markings on the wings and tail. She knew there was a group of six B-17's coming in, but this was more like fifty or sixty planes. When she heard the first crashing explosion of a direct hit, she realized what was going on.

"We're under attack!" She screamed at Higs as both women ran for cover next to the hangar. Most of the women from their squadron were inside the hangar. A few came running outside.

Multiple explosions were heard back-to-back-to-back. Thick fireballs full of shrapnel rose three-hundred feet into the blue sky, filling it with black smoke so thick the ships in Battleship Row could barely be seen.

"Who the hell is that shooting at us?!" Patterson yelled over the explosions.

"Jap bombers!" Charley yelled back. She was trying to get a head count of her squadron when another group of planes flew over. "Take cover!"

The second set of planes were Japanese Zeros. They flew low over the airfield on the island with their machine guns spitting fire, strafing the neatly parked planes and vehicles full of holes outside of the hangars. A handful of bombers followed, dropping bombs all over the airstrip and close to the hangars.

Airmen and aircrew members were running all over in confusion and fear, diving for some semblance of shelter as planes and trucks exploded all around them from the rain of bullets from the next strafing run of planes overhead.

Charley started running from the shelter of the hangar when she heard the loud whine of an incoming bomb.

"Get out of the hangar!" she shouted.

The bomb whirled, screaming and howling in the air directly overhead. She could clearly see the cylindrical shape, the fins, even the white markings on the side as it sped closer and closer. It finally reached its target less than twenty-five feet from her. It passed through hangar two with a loud crash and detonated with a violent explosion that tossed the building off the ground and threw her five feet into the air. The building groaned and collapsed with flames licking the edges. Charley was laying on her back covered in dirt and shrapnel when she opened her eyes. The bright blue sky was replaced by billowing black smoke in every direction. She jumped up when she heard the faint humming of more planes in the distance. All of the planes in her vicinity were bullet-scarred or smoldering and blown apart.

"Higs!" Charley shouted, wiping away blood pouring from cuts on her forehead and chin.

"Over here!" Higs shouted from thirty feet away.

"Come on!" Charley ran through the smoke and flames to the Armory building fifty yards away. She and Higs kicked the door in and grabbed as many thirty and fifty caliber machine guns as they could carry. Two other aircrew members went in behind them and grabbed canisters full of ammo.

"Get to the pit as fast as you can!" Charley yelled.

Charley and Higs were running towards the gun pit made of sandbags, out in the open on the side of the airstrip closest to the hangars, when they heard screaming and shouting. Charley passed off the guns she was carrying and went towards the sound as Higs continued on with the others and began loading the guns as fast as they could. A few more members of Charley's squadron and some of the airmen from nearby hangars grabbed guns and took cover wherever they could.

Charley finally found the source of the screaming. Lt. Carl Davis was covered in blood from shrapnel cuts and had burns and broken bones sticking out of his legs. He was laying partly under one of the Wildcat Fighter planes that had been blown apart and was now smoldering. The plane had been blown up while he was trying to climb inside. He was screaming in pain.

"Help me, please!" he begged.

Charley had no idea how bad he was injured and the hum of the planes was getting closer and closer. She grabbed him under his arm pits and pulled as hard as she could.

"My legs! My legs!" he shrieked and cried out as she pulled him out from under the burning plane.

The pit was clearly too far away to drag him so she maneuvered around the burning plane to a destroyed truck that was flipped on its side from a nearby bomb and thankfully not on fire. She pulled him against it and took her jacket off. Tearing it into strips, she placed them over the huge cuts across his chest and abdomen and peered down at his mangled legs. His flight suit pants were burnt and glued to his skin and she could see the white bones sticking out of both legs.

46

"I'll be right back," she yelled and took off running in the opposite direction. When she reached the pit, she grabbed two guns and a metal ammo box. She ran back behind the truck just as the planes were crossing overhead.

Charley placed one of the machine guns up on the side of the truck and began firing when she saw the planes flying towards her through the thick smoke clouds. Beside her, plane shrapnel was flying all around from exploding planes and strafing bullets were digging into the ground. Men all around were wounded, and then wounded again from the non-stop explosions and machine gun raining from the sky.

The low-flying light-grey planes with big red circles on the wings kept coming and she kept shooting, barely slowing down enough to wipe the blood from her eyes. She wouldn't give up, wouldn't abandon her station, wouldn't quit trying to give back some of the destruction the Japanese planes were intent on raining down on everything and everyone around her. When she noticed smoke billowing from one of the Zeros over-head, she smiled, watching it fly lower and lower until it plummeted to the ground, with a fireball rising a hundred feet into the air. She heard cheering and pumped her fist in the air when she saw Army Air Force planes in a dog fight above them. She and the others laid down thousands of rounds of cover fire as they watched one more Zero hit the ground in flames.

When the planes finally cleared, Charley gathered the members of her squad that she could find and began searching through the planes to see if they get could any of them off the ground in case the Japanese planes returned.

"There's nothing," Charley yelled.

"Everything's blown to pieces, God damn it!" Higs yelled back.

"Patterson, stay with the guns. Higs, we need to go find the rest of the squadron and get Lt. Davis to the dispensary if it's even still standing."

Charley only had a head count for eight of her fifteen women, half of which were seriously injured. She feared the worst when she looked at the flaming hangar. They were happy to see four of the women helping some of the aircrew from the fighter squadron who were connecting hoses to try and put out the fires in the hangars that were still standing.

"Who's missing?" Charley said.

Higs did a mental roster check. "I haven't seen Cpl. Lowe, Pvt. Edwin, and Pvt. Geiger."

"Have any of you seen these three?" Charley asked the four women.

"Oh no, not Shirley. She was in hangar two. I saw her working in the cockpit of a bomber when we heard the first explosion," one of the corporals said as tears began flowing down her face. "We were the last ones to come out before it blew apart. She wasn't with us."

"Okay, we'll look for her. What about the others?"

"Edwin and Geiger are over here," Higs shouted. "Edwin's got a broken arm and shrapnel wounds."

Charley and Higs tried to get near the collapsed hangar but the flames were covering every entrance point. The building was just a mangled heap of burning metal.

"No. We have to get her out," Higs screamed.

"I'm sorry," Charley saluted the pile, went to pull the garrison cap from her head and realized it was no longer there. She must have lost it during the raid. She held her hand over her heart as a few tears fell, smearing with the blood and dirt on her cheeks and chin. "Be with God, Cpl. Lowe."

"No. No. No. She's not gone. We can get her," Higs cried and dropped to her knees.

Charley put her hand on her shoulder. "Stand-up, Sgt. Higginbotham. Honor her the way she would want to be honored, the way she should be honored. She was an Army Air Force Aircrew member and a damn good one."

Higs stood up and saluted. The other members of the squadron that were able to, walked up behind them and stood at attention, saluting the burning pile in silence.

Charley turned around and cleared her throat. "We need to get this fire under control. There is a body in there that will need to be recovered and sent home to a family," she said solemnly.

A truck came barreling towards them skidding to a stop before crashing into one of the smoldering planes.

"We need help!" the guy in the passenger seat yelled when he jumped out. "There are men trapped in the ships. We need tools to drill through the hull of a ship. There are men trapped and suffocating!"

Charley ran to the hangar that was still standing and prayed it stayed up with all of the holes littering it. She loaded the truck with drills, jack-hammers, and other heavy equipment tools.

"Higs, grab as many tools as you can fit in this truck. The rest of you stay and get this fire out. Patterson, you've just been promoted to Sergeant. You're in charge of getting this fire out and recovering Cpl. Lowe's remains."

Charley and Higs climbed into the back of the truck with two other women. The rest were either putting out the fire or lying on the ground, too injured to move. They held on tightly as the truck bounced over huge craters and pot holes the bombs and bullets had left in the roads.

"You're being promoted also. Congratulations, Staff Sergeant," Charley said. "Who knows where we go from here. We're already in hell." She could see nothing but blackness as they neared battleship row.

"Do you guys have an extra truck you can send back? We have a gravely injured airman back there that needs medical attention," Charley said to one of the men next to her.

"Yes, we'll send a truck back as soon as we drop you ladies off at the dock."

Chapter Six

The trucked rounded the corner and all Charley could see was thick black smoke. The battleships were all mangled and on fire. Some were on their sides or capsized while others were sunk in their mooring. They were all surrounded by burning oil slicks on the water's surface. Sailors were screaming and burning as they swam through the oil slicks littered with floating bodies.

"Oh my god," she whispered.

The Arizona was blown to pieces and sunk with most of the crew still inside. The ship was completely unrecognizable and covered in flames so thick no one could get close to it. In the distance, the Oklahoma's starboard side was above the water with part of her keel exposed.

"Come on!" one of the guys yelled when the truck screeched to a halt.

Charley and the squad members she'd brought grabbed their tools and rushed down to the row boats.

"There are men trapped in the Oklahoma!" one of the rowers shouted.

Other rowboats were all around them, pulling the sailors that were still alive from the burning water. The air was black as night and thick with sulfur and the sickening smell of burnt oil.

Charley watched Higs wipe a tear from her cheek just before the rowboat bounced against the hull of the ship. A dozen sailors and yard workers were clambering all over the hull with flashlights trying to see in the dark smoke and struggling to figure out a way in.

Charley and Higs climbed up onto the keel with their tools looking for some sort of order in the chaos.

"We can hear them banging on the bulkhead in two spots," one of the sailors said, grabbing some of the tools from the women and directing them to the location of the last pinging sounds.

"Higs, go find out how to get an airline out here," Charley said, pointing at the jackhammer and air drills lying by her feet.

"We got it coming," one of the sailors replied.

Charley breathed in the rancid air and coughed. She saw the Arizona in the distance, still smoldering with huge orange flames and black smoke filled with soot. The water around her was so thick with oil it was like rowing or swimming through tar.

"They're stuck in air pockets in the engine room, but it's only a matter of time before the water starts coming in on them." A sailor standing next to Charley sighed and scratched his hairline. The sound of the pinging inside the ship was echoing on the outside with a cadence that reminded Charley of her own heartbeat.

"Looks like you're bleeding pretty good there," he said to her.

"I'm fine." Charley wiped the blood from her face on the sleeve of her t-shirt just as the rowboat arrived with the airlines.

Charley and Higs went to work hooking up the lines to the air tools and looking for the best place to begin drilling.

***

After a couple of hours drilling into the hull, Charley and Higs were relieved of duty so they could go be with their squadron. They were surprised to see the dispensary still standing when they stopped by. Most of the buildings around it were crumbled to pieces. Most of the dispensary's white walls were covered with strafing lines, but surprisingly no bombs had hit it directly.

They walked past rows and rows of men laying outside on the ground with the red letter 'F' for fatal in the middle of their foreheads. They were severely burned or mangled beyond recognition and were all deceased. Once they got inside, they saw more men with red letters laying on gurneys or sitting in chairs. Most of them had 'M's in the middle of their foreheads indicating they'd been given morphine.

"My god," Higs said, softly covering her face and mouth to quell the stench of burnt flesh.

Charley looked around for someone that appeared to be in-charge. Finally, she stopped a nurse in the hallway.

"If you're not dying go back to your unit," the nurse said as she continued walking.

Charley followed her. "I'm trying to check on someone who was brought in and find out where the designated morgue is."

"Charley!" a soft voice yelled from the other end of the hallway over the disarray.

Charley looked all around and just about fell over when the petite woman dove into her arms. Charley held her tightly before letting go and backing away.

"Oh my god, I'm so glad you're okay. I was so worried. The whole damn island is on fire and blown to bits. These sailors, god help me, they're burned so bad all we can do is give them morphine and cut the dead skin off. I've never seen anything like it in my life. Every other patient I see dies before I can get back to them. Bodies are stacking up everywhere. I thought...I kept waiting to see you get thrown into the pile," Audrey wiped the few tears from her eyes.

Charley put her hands on Audrey's shoulders. "I'm here. I'm fine, a little bloody, but I'll live."

Audrey reached up and wiped the blood from Charley's face. "You need stitches again, Major," she smiled.

"I know, but I can wait. I'm actually looking for an airmen that was badly injured and should've been brought in a couple hours ago."

"Was he brought here or taken over to the hospital?"

"I don't know. We've been out on the Oklahoma trying to cut holes in the hull. It's on its side with men trapped inside."

"Oh my god. It just keeps getting worse and worse."

"The water is completely on fire and full of burning bodies. It's not going to end anytime soon unfortunately," Higs said.

"Why would they do this to us?" Audrey sighed.

"I have no idea, but hopefully those bastards don't come back." Higs coughed up some of the soot she'd inhaled while out in battleship row.

"Do you know what the Medical Corps is using as a morgue?"

"I have no idea. We have about forty dead bodies so far and they keep stacking up. Some of them barely had any clothes on. There's no way to I.D. anyone. I've assisted on more surgeries this morning than my whole career totaled. The only thing we can do is try and make people comfortable. We're not a hospital. I heard the hospital is worse off than we are. Someone said they've had no power for over an hour, but I think it's back up now. If this is what hell is like, I don't ever want to go there again."

"I don't think hell is this brutal," Charley said, looking around at the screaming burn victims on gurneys littering the walls of the hallway.

Audrey looked from Charley to Higs and peered around them. "Where's Patterson?"

"She's fine. She actually should've come by here by now. We lost one of our squadron members and Patterson was supposed to retrieve her body. That's who I'm looking for. I need to make sure she is identified correctly. I will contact her next of kin myself."

"I'm sorry," Audrey said.

"Nurse Sutton, you're needed in surgery and it's time for bandage checks," Dr. Olsen said as he walked by them.

"I need to get back to my squadron. I'll check in with you in a day or so," Charley said.

"Please be safe out there," Audrey said, squeezing her hand.

"Higs, I'll let Fran know I saw you." She winked and walked away.

Charley was surprised to see most of her squadron near the crumbled hangar when she pulled up in the yard truck she had borrowed. There was still smoke coming from the rubble, but the fire was out.

"Major," Patterson stood at attention and saluted. Charley returned the salute.

"Did Lt. Davis get picked up?"

"Yes, ma'am. I believe they took him to the hospital on the mainland."

"Good. What about Cpl. Lowe? Have her remains been recovered?"

"We just extinguished the fire a few minutes before you arrived. I didn't think it was ever going to stop burning. It's still smoldering in some areas," Patterson said.

"Higs, see if you can find some rope. I think we can pull the roof back with the truck."

Charley backed the truck up next to the largest chuck of the metal roof and waited for Higs to return with rope.

"This is all I could find," Higs said, holding up extension cords and air hose lines.

"That'll work. Loop it around those metal rods and tie it to the frame not the bumper and get the hell out of the way." Charley climbed back into the yard truck and started it up.

Higs gave the thumbs up and Charley put the truck in gear. She eased out the clutch and felt the tug of the lines as she pressed the gas. The rear tires of the truck began squealing from the weight and she pressed the gas harder. Slowly, the metal fragments of the roof began sliding away, revealing the crumbled ruins underneath it.

Charley stopped the truck and went to inspect the remainder of the building.

"There's the plane," Patterson yelled.

Charley stuck her bare hand on the rubble to check the heat. It was warm to the touch, but not enough to burn so she climbed up on top of the pile and crawled the fifteen yards back to what appeared to be the fuselage of the bomber.

"Get a couple of pry bars," she yelled.

Higs and two of the squad members ran over to the hangar that was still standing and returned with large metal rods. Higs and Patterson crawled over to Charley.

"We have to get this large slab out of the way." She pointed to the concrete slab from the floor that had blown up over the top of the plane.

All three women pried with all of their weight and moved the slab enough to see the cockpit of the plane. Cpl. Shirley Lowe's body was slumped over the stick and against the controls. It looked like she was probably crushed on impact. She was badly burned, probably when the fuel tank of the bomber caught fire.

Charley backed away. Running a hand through her hair she cleared her throat, and recited the Lord's Prayer. Higs and Patterson joined in solemnly.

"Higs, go find something to use as a gurney. Patterson, find something to cover her with. No one else needs to see her like this," Charley exclaimed.

A few minutes later the women of the squadron stood at attention saluting with a few airmen from the flight squadron standing with them as Cpl. Lowe's body was carried out of the wreckage.

Chapter Seven

Five days later, Charley was standing next to one of the planes her squadron was trying to resurrect. So far, they'd gotten two pursuits and one bomber back in flying condition. She'd also fixed the strafing damage on her Jeep and had it running. The airbase was on red alert status around the clock and the entire island was blacked out at night in case of another attack. All of the buildings had black curtains up at night and the curfew was dark so there was no reason for anyone to be out. This cut Charley's squadron's work time in half since they couldn't work after dark.

Battleship Row was still covered in dark thick smoke and the *Arizona* was still burning. The yard workers had finally retrieved over thirty men from the *Oklahoma*, but had been unable to get to the others. Their pings had finally silenced.

Charley was staring up at the fading sky about to close up shop for the night when she heard the crunch of tires on the strafed and pitted concrete. She turned to see a car in the distance. A silhouetted figure got out and the car drove away. Charley pulled the bent doors of the hangar together and clicked the lock in place. She laughed when she saw the giant crater sized holes in the side of the hangar covered by plywood. Closing and locking the doors was almost comical, but it was protocol.

"I was hoping I'd catch you before you left for the day," Audrey said.

"I stayed later than I should have. I was on the phone trying to coordinate a flight off the island for Cpl. Lowe's remains. Her family wants her buried at home," Charley tugged on the lock to make sure it was secure. "The rest of my squadron left about an hour ago."

"I'm sorry I haven't seen you in days. I've literally been working eight hours on and eight hours off shifts around the clock, changing bandages and soaking the most severe patients in saltwater baths. It's horrible. I can't get the screaming out of my head and I think the smell of burnt flesh is forever stuck in my hair."

"Has it gotten any better over there?" Charley asked.

"Not really. We've been spraying tannic acid solution on the burns and cutting off the dead skin with scissors. I spent most of last night crying with some of the patients that just wanted someone to hold their hand and sit with them. They're in severe pain and they're scared. Sixty percent of the patients we saw on Sunday passed away either that day or the day after. We ran out of blood Sunday night and were using flashlights to draw blood from sailors and airmen that showed up to donate. At one point we were literally drawing the blood into Coke bottles because it was so dark we couldn't find the glass cartridges."

Charley pulled the keys from her pocket and re-opened the lock, pushing the doors apart just enough to squeeze inside. She waved Audrey inside and slid the doors closed. She fumbled around looking for the flashlight she knew was close to the door. She found it and flicked the switch. The light cast a soft glow, illuminating the hangar with just enough light for Audrey to see Charley walking towards her.

Charley put her hands on Audrey's waist and pulled her against her. She wrapped her arms around her, holding her tightly. She bent her head, pressing her lips to Audrey's. Audrey melted into her arms, relaxing against the body holding her up as she tasted the mouth she so desperately craved. They kissed each other fervently, barely pausing to breathe, not knowing if this would be the last time they would ever see each other.

Audrey's hips moved against Charley's on their own accord and Charley backed her up against the plane behind them.

"We can't do this, not here. It's dirty and it smells," Charley panted, pulling away from Audrey.

Audrey ran her hand up the front of Charley's uniform jacket to her soft cheek.

"I don't care where we are. I want to be with you, Charley," she pleaded.

"Have you ever been in a bomber?" Charley asked, grabbing her hand and walking her over to the light grey Bolo sitting in the middle of the hangar, awaiting repairs to the wings and tail.

"No," Audrey said.

Charley opened the access door behind the wing and pulled the step stool over. She motioned for Audrey and helped her climb up inside the fuselage. Charley climbed inside behind her and pulled the door partly closed. She spanned the light around the tight space, noting the slightly open space behind the crew seats.

"It's not the cleanest or roomiest place..."

Audrey pressed her fingers to Charley's mouth and began unbuttoning her dress with the other. Charley playfully bit and licked the fingers while removing her jacket and boots. She placed her jacket behind Audrey so she would have something between her and the metal floor of the plane.

Audrey lied back, pulling Charley down on top of her. Charley covered the top of her chest and neck in soft kisses, moving lower to the opening of the dress, revealing the soft skin of her pale breasts and pink nipples. The small light barely projected enough light to see anything, but Audrey's nude body was an image permanently burned into her mind.

"Touch me, Charley," Audrey whispered, pulling Charley's t-shirt over her head.

Charley ran her hand up Audrey's thigh under her dress and pulled her panties down to her ankles. Audrey kicked out of them, flinging them against the small crew window over the wing. Charley's fingers brushed the delicate wet folds. Audrey shifted her position to spread her legs further when Charley's finger tips passed over her entrance. Charley moved her fingers in lazy teasing circles, mimicking the motion with her mouth on Audrey's breasts. She flicked her tongue over Audrey's pink nipple every time her finger's swept over her clit.

Audrey ran her nails over Charley's back, moaning loudly as two fingers slid inside of her. Her hips swayed with every thrust of Charley's fingers, pushing them deeper. Charley moved her mouth from Audrey's breasts to the side of her neck, kissing a lazy path before running her tongue around Audrey's lips.

Audrey reached down between their connected bodies, opening the button and unzipping Charley's pants. Charley's hips rose up enough to answer her request. Audrey slipped her hand under the waistband of Charley's underwear through the patch of hair to the wet center she knew was begging to be touched. Charley's hips jerked with the first pass of Audrey's fingers over her clit. She settled into a comfortable position and began riding Audrey's fingers, sliding back and forth over them with every thrust of her fingers inside the other woman.

Charley knew it wouldn't be long. She was working on overload and had been running on pure adrenaline for the past three days. Her body was ready to implode from sheer exhaustion. She groaned loudly, quivering as the orgasm passed over her in multiple waves.

"Oh Charley...oh my..." Audrey cried out, clinching tightly around the fingers inside of her. She rode her hips back and forth until she could no longer move. She lay breathless on the floor of the Bolo bomber covered in a light sheen of sweat with her breasts and hips exposed to the warm air. She smiled and laughed.

"What's so funny?" Charley was lying next to her, smashed against the curve of the fuselage, topless with her pants open and pushed down slightly.

"This." Audrey fanned her hand over them. "We're indecently exposed and squished on the floor inside of a grungy, stinky, military plane full of bullet holes. Did I mention we're also at war?"

Charley chuckled and shook her head. "I should probably get you to your barracks before they send out a search party."

"What about you? I heard your barracks were flattened."

"Yeah, part of the building was and it's unsafe so we're bunking with the Navy guys over at the yard. They're the float plane mechanics and pilots. We are crammed into one small room with racks down both walls. It's not exactly ideal, but at this point we will take what we can get."

"And the back of this plane is...ideal?" Audrey teased and tapped on the metal next to her head.

"Something like that." Charley bent her head and kissed her.

***

Charley snuck into her rack an hour later. She hadn't been able to resist making love to Audrey once more. Plus, she'd had to drive around the island with no lights because of the blackout so she'd driven slowly. Her Jeep had bounced all over the potholes and bomb craters.

She tossed her jacket on her footlocker, placed her boots next to it, careful not to make any noise, and climbed into her small rack.

"Coming in a little late huh, Major?" Higs said from the next bed over.

Charley shook her head. She hated being in such cramped quarters. There were two rows with ten double racks down each side. Charley's squadron only fifteen women plus herself, well fourteen now that Cpl. Lowe was gone, and five of them were in the hospital recovering from injuries. With all of the open beds, Higs just had to take the one directly next to hers and she snored so that made it worse.

"Go to sleep, Higs. That's an order," Charley whispered harshly and rolled over to get away from the spring poking her in the back.

"Don't be a sourpuss," Higs whispered. "I wish I could stay out for hours after lights out," she mumbled to herself.

"Damn it, SSgt. Higginbotham. Go to sleep and mind your own business before I demote you," Charley hissed.

"Grouch," Higs huffed and rolled over.

Chapter Eight

Charley had just returned from having lunch in what remained of the mess hall. She was tired from barely sleeping the night before. Staying out late then spending the night tossing and turning trying to avoid springs jabbing her sides and back made for a rough morning. The nasty black coffee she was drinking wasn't mixing well with her rubber chicken lunch, and she'd also had an impromptu meeting at Hickam Airbase with the Pacific Fleet Lieutenant Colonel.

"Is that Mohawk ready or are you still working on it?" Higs asked.

"I don't know. Check the log," Charley snapped and threw her hands up.

"You've been a major grump all day." Higs stormed over to log sheet.

"The Mohawk and that yard truck are both good to go. The Bolo needs a new wing panel on this side." Charley pointed. "Try to get those two Mohawks started that are sitting outside. We need to get as many of these planes flight ready as we can just in case those bastards come back." Charley tossed her coffee in the trash and drove over to their temporary barracks to change into her utility uniform so she could go back to work, but decided to drive around and clear her head instead.

***

Charley returned to the hangar and paced back and forth on the battered concrete next to her Jeep. The meeting with Lt. Col. Mayburn had been worse than she'd expected. Due to the sudden attack on Pearl Harbor they were now stationed in the 'hot zone' and female squadrons and units were not permitted to be stationed in 'hot zones', so they were being reassigned and flying out at 0800. She still needed to brief her squadron.

Charley walked inside and picked up a few stray tools from the floor. She moved to place the tools in the toolbox she was working out of and stumbled almost dropping them on her feet when she saw the light pink panties lying on top of her tools. She looked around and Higs was standing a few feet away casually tossing a wrench in the air and grinning.

"Care to explain why I found those in the Bolo?" Higs was standing there with this grin on her face that made her look like she'd just found the Holy Grail and was ready to barter a trade for the location.

Charley's back was ramrod straight. She cleared her throat. "Who said those belong to me?"

Higs laughed. "Oh, I know they aren't yours. The question is, whose are they? And how did they end up in one of our planes?"

Charley put the panties in the trashcan and rearranged it so they weren't visible. She turned back towards Higs, shrugged nonchalantly, and began walking away.

"You know, I'm not the only one that saw them," Higs stated.

Charley swallowed the lump in her throat and spun around.

"Who..."

"I am however, the only one that knows you came in after midnight."

"Fine, Higs, you got me. I was sitting in the back of the Bolo last night wearing frilly pink panties while working on the strafing damage." Charley mock-fanned herself.

Higs laughed hysterically. "Oh please."

"Any more questions?" Charley asked.

"Were you working on...I mean with...Audrey?"

Charley shook her head. "Such a dirty mind for a young lady," she chided.

Higs laughed again, rolling her eyes.

"Oh by the way, I went to the dispensary this morning to see if they needed anymore blood since I heard they were rationing what they did have. Anyway, the head nurse asked me if your itch was gone and wanted to know if I had it too? What the hell is that all about?"

Charley snickered. "I forgot about that. I needed an excuse to get the nurses out the night we went to the picture show. I said I had an inconspicuous itch and it was spreading to my squadron."

"Oh that's funny. Now she thinks we all have your itch."

"You won't have to see her again, so don't worry about it."

"What do you mean?" Higs asked.

Charley nodded towards the door and Higs followed her outside.

"My meeting this morning was to inform me that we're being reassigned because Pearl is now a 'hot zone'."

"Oh no. Where are they shipping us to?"

"Actually, we're staying with the Pacific Fleet. Our squadron is being stationed in the Midway Islands."

"Isn't that close by? What's the point of that?"

"I know it's stupid, but apparently Midway isn't near the war. We leave at 0800 on a transport plane."

"How nice." Higs kicked the side of the hangar with her booted foot.

"Brief the squad and head back to the barracks. We need to pack up and get ready to fly out."

"What about our work for the day?"

"It's not my problem anymore. Tell the squad I'll answer any questions that I can when I get there." Charley climbed into the Jeep.

"Wait, do you want to return something to Audrey?" Higs nodded towards the hangar insinuating she take the panties with her.

Charley started the Jeep and drove off without saying anything.

* * *

The dispensary was still buzzing with injured sailors and nurses running around with their nurse caps on fire, trying to stay ahead of the patient list. Charley stopped Dr. Olsen in the hallway and asked him to point her in Audrey's direction. He was reluctant to at first, which she found odd, but he finally said she was in the area that they'd set up as a surgery ward. Charley walked briskly down the hall careful to avoid the gurneys with injured sailors that still lined the halls.

"Hey!" Audrey said when she walked out of a room and saw Charley walking towards her in her Dress Uniform. She cleared her throat. "What can I do for you, Maj. Hayes?"

"Can you talk? I hate to come here like this, but I don't have much time."

"Is everything okay?"

"Yes and no."

"Let me get Fran to cover for me. I'll meet you outside." Audrey went back into the room she had come out of and Charley walked back towards the front of the building.

When Audrey came outside, she saw Charley sitting on a broken bench staring at the strafing lines on the side of the building.

"What's wrong?" she said when she stopped in front of her.

"First of all, Higs found your panties in the Bolo today."

"Oh no!" Audrey gasped.

"Are you...Is that what..." Audrey covered her mouth with her hand. "Are you being kicked out..."

"No. No. It's fine. I'm lucky she was the one that found them," Charley said.

"I'm so sorry. I was careless."

"We both were," she sighed. "That's not the real reason I'm here." Charley stood and motioned for Audrey to sit on the partial bench.

"My squadron is being reassigned. We fly out in the morning. I just found out, but I knew it would happen.

The Army Air Force doesn't allow women to serve near 'hot zones' which is stupid, but it's the rules. Since this base was blown to bits a week ago it's now a 'hot zone'."

"That's crazy. Where will you go?"

"We're staying in the Pacific Fleet, but that's all I know."

"When will I see you again?"

"Audrey, we're at war. Who knows how long it will last or where we will both end up. I still have three more years and if the war isn't over by then who knows how many more. This is a career for me anyway so I plan to re-sign when my time is up. You and I, it never would've lasted past this island anyway."

"Don't say that, Charley. We can write and see each other down the road. Please don't say goodbye." Audrey wiped the tears that began falling from her eyes.

"I care about you, but this is the best thing for both of us," Charley put her hand on Audrey's shoulder.

"Charley..." Audrey grabbed her hand when she moved to walk away. "Please be safe. I'll worry about you and wonder where you are for the rest of my life," she cried.

"I'll be fine. Take care of yourself and get the hell away from this war as soon as you can." Charley squeezed her hand. "Goodbye, Audrey."

Chapter Nine

Charley watched Pearl Harbor disappear from her line of sight through the window over the wing as the C-46 Commando ascended above the clouds in the beginning of their eight-hour flight to the Midway Islands. She hated leaving two crew members behind, but their injuries were bad enough to get them medals and a nice 'thank you' letter from the government as they were discharged and easily replaced by two more women standing in line behind them now that the country was at war. Her squadron was now down to twelve members with two of them still licking their wounds. She wasn't exactly up to par herself with stitches in her hairline above her forehead, plus the numerous cuts, scrapes, and bruises all over her body.

"Why didn't they send us over on a ship instead of cramming us in here?" Higs yelled over the loud buzz of the engines.

Charley shrugged. She had the same feeling. The plane they were on was an Army Air Force Transport plane and was capable of carrying over forty troops at any given time, but it also doubled as a cargo plane when needed. In its current state, the plane was covering both

71

roles. The women were squished into three rows of side-by-side seats behind the pilots with a center aisle and the remainder of the plane was full of cargo crates with miscellaneous parts, food, and any other necessities the airmen and sailors serving on the island had requested.

"I bet there are hotdogs made from pig lips in one of those crates back there sitting in a more comfortable position than I am right now." Higs tried to stretch her short legs and failed miserably when her feet hit a barrier under the seat in front of her. She looked over at the slightly taller Major sitting next to her and huffed. Charley hadn't moved a muscle since they'd taken off and seemed surprisingly comfortable in her compressed state.

"Whoever said 'misery loves company' lied through his teeth. Now, shut up and sleep or something. You're making my hair turn grey," Charley sneered, closing her eyes. She had barely slept the night before. Saying goodbye to Audrey had turned out to be much more difficult than she'd anticipated. She didn't think it was love, but then again she'd never cared for anyone the way she cared for her. It didn't really matter now, it was over and she would never see her again anyway.

When the plane bounced its landing on the runway, Charley was jolted awake in her seat. She sat up, peering out the window. The sun was shining off the sand dunes and blue ocean water behind the buildings. They were on Eastern Island which was a very small island completely consumed by Naval Air Station Midway, their home for the next however many months the Army Air Force decided to keep them there.

"This is it?" Patterson looked around when she stepped out of the plane.

"Welcome to NAS Midway, ladies. Take it all in. This is the Army Air Force's idea of roughing it. There's no mainland to go to. Nothing but a bunch of airmen and sailors with nothing but time on their hands. Keep a close watch on each other and never go out alone, day or night." Charley was standing in front of her squadron with her shoulders squared and her superior officer face on.

"How long are we here?" Higs asked.

"Until the Lieutenant Colonel says so," Charley said, watching a small Jeep barreling towards them. It reminded her of the one she had at Ford Island.

"You must be Maj. Hayes," the man said as he jumped out, barely stopping the vehicle beforehand.

"That's correct. This is my squadron." Charley stood at attention and saluted him along with all of the women standing behind her.

"I'm Col. James Harvey. I'm the CO for the Army Air Force Fighter Group. This is Sand Island. It's three square miles and one of two islands that together make up the Naval Air Station. We have a fighter squadron and a bomber squadron stationed here. They are over on Eastern Island. You will be working with my guys, servicing and repairing our fleet. We also work closely with the Navy and Marine Corps. Flight Squadrons that are assigned to the airbase so you may have to service their planes from time to time. You're squadron is assigned to hangar four which is a fairly large building on the edge of the main runway. The only other hangar on this island is for the Navy sea planes. There are two hangars on Eastern Island and you may be sent over occasionally for repairs on planes that can't make the mile wide flight between islands. Also, you'll be staying in unused officer's quarters in building ten with its own facilities. Only drink water from the kitchen sink. Both islands use saltwater that is somewhat cleansed so it's more like brackish water. Technically, there is no fresh water here. There is a mess hall that serves three meals a day, a free movie house, and a gymnasium. Fishing is pretty much everyone's past-time here, unless you get in good with the Navy guys. Some of them go diving on the backside of the islands where there is a volcanic reef." He turned to get back in the Jeep. "Oh and there is no private transportation available, but there are yard trucks that ride all over, just hitch a ride on one of them. You can rent bicycles too if you'd like. Here comes your truck now. The driver knows where to take you. Get settled in this evening and I'll see you at 0700 for a quick briefing. Welcome to Midway, ladies."

When he drove away, Charley let out the breath she'd been holding and her shoulders deflated. She silently prayed their stay on the island wouldn't be very long.

"This sucks," Patterson kicked the ground with her boot and climbed into the back of the yard truck.

"No shit," Higs added, following her inside.

Charley jumped up in the cab and rode with the driver who casually saluted her as if it wasn't necessary. She gritted her teeth and stared through the windshield as the truck sputtered and bounced along the widest section of the island and clamored to a stop next to a group of barracks.

Charley jumped out, slung her bag over her shoulder, and led the women to their new home. Building ten wasn't fabulous and most definitely wasn't five-star accommodations, but each woman once again had her own closet-sized private room. They were lucky to have running water even it if was semi-salty. There were only four bathrooms, which would definitely make for some time shuffling in the mornings.

"How long are we here again?" Higs asked, standing in the doorway of the room across the hall.

Charley tossed her bag on the bed and shut her door. She didn't want to be there any more than anyone else, but this was what she'd signed on for. She was doing what she loved, fixing things. She'd sleep in a tent full of sand with only a canteen of water to wash with if it meant she could wear an Army uniform and work with planes. She wasn't, however, thrilled about being strafed or having bombs dropped on her head.

***

Christmas had come and gone and New Year's was a few days away. Charley was elbow deep in the engine compartment of a Marine Corps F2-A Buffalo fighter fixing a hydraulic line. She was just about finished when she paused and wiped the sweat from her brow. She looked out the open hangar doors at the twenty planes parked outside on the tarmac. Half of her squadron was outside in the sun, working on planes because the workload was too large for just one hangar. They were the direct service squadron for two bomber squadrons with close to thirty planes in total. Plus, they were the second-hand service squadron for the Navy and Marine Corps fighters when their service squadrons were backed up due to their fleet of over a hundred planes.

"New station, new island, new plane models, same old men and superior bullshit," Higs huffed, walking past Charley to her toolbox.

"Tell me how you really feel." Charley laughed.

"Are they ever going to realize we are not here to do everyone's bitch work? I mean seriously. Those squids need to either learn how to work on their own planes or find something else to do. That Dauntless bomber I've been working on all day is a perfectly fine plane with water in the oil because some dipshit tried to put water in an air-cooled engine," Higs growled.

"Unfortunately, as a Service Squadron, we are generalized which means we play nice and work on whatever they bring us."

"We're working twelve hour days because they have too many planes and not enough service personnel to keep up with them."

"I won't argue with that, but it's not like we have any control over it." Charley stuffed her wrenches into her back pocket and climbed down the ladder. "Go cool off. The day is almost over anyway."

"What about my plane? I'm not finished draining all of the oil."

"The choice is yours, take it or leave it. Either way, someone has to finish that plane."

"I've got it. Put it on the test flight schedule for tomorrow morning." Higs walked back outside towards the heavy bomber.

Just before dark, the women gathered around waiting for the yard truck to come by and take them home for the night. Charley hated relying on someone else for transportation.

"The hell with this, I'm walking back," Higs said.

"Me too." Patterson said.

"Neither of you are walking anywhere. The truck is over there." Charley pointed and pulled Higs aside.

"Damn it, Higs, you need to lead by example. If you let these girls see you giving into the assholes then they will think that's what they are supposed to do. We are soldiers stationed here just like everyone else and we need to demand the same respect. Now, get your panties out of a wad and get your ass into the back of that truck." Charley shook her head and sighed before climbing into the cab of the truck.

"Good evening, Major."

Charley looked at the young pipsqueak sitting behind the wheel with a big grin on his face.

"Stop the truck."

"Excuse me?"

"You heard me, stop the god damn truck," Charley yelled.

The heavy truck lurched to a halt.

"Get out," she ordered.

When the young man climbed out of the truck Charley was already standing by his door.

"The next time you deliberately pick my squadron up late I will tie you to the command flag pole at half-staff by the skin of your balls! Now, march your ass to the back of this truck and apologize to these soldiers for purposely making their long day that much longer. If you haven't noticed, our country is at war. There is a reason these women are stationed here. They possess desirable skills that are critical in keeping planes in the air so people like you aren't attacked when the enemy comes knocking on your door. Let me ask you this, where were you when Pearl Harbor was blown to bits? These women were right in the middle of it, being strafed and bombed just like all of the men." Charley pointed to the back of the truck. "This is what is left of our squadron. The rest are in the hospital and one was sent home in a box. So, the next time you think we are just a bunch of useless women wasting your time, you remember why we are here and the purpose we serve and you will address our ranks with the respect they deserve." Charley took a step back.

He immediately saluted her and Charley nodded and returned the salute. She watched as he walked to the back of the truck apologizing and promising to be on time every shift.

Chapter Ten

Charley was laying on the small bed in her room reading a repair manual for the TBF Avenger. It was a new torpedo bomber in the Navy's carrier fleet and she hadn't had the opportunity to work on one of these beautiful ladies yet and she wanted to be prepared. Besides, it was New Year's Eve and she had nothing else to do. Living on Midway Island was nothing like living on Ford Island where you could take the ferry over to the mainland and have somewhat of a normal evening away from the base with a tease of civilian life. She ignored the knock on her door and continued reading.

"Open up, Major. I know you're in there," Higs shouted from the other side of the door.

"Go away."

"Either you come out or I'm coming in."

Charley heard the door knob jingle. Rolling her eyes, she set the book on her bed and got up.

"What do you want?" Charley said, flinging open the door.

"It's New Year's Eve and you're sitting in here like a hermit. Come celebrate."

"I'm perfectly fine right here."

Higs moved past her to grab the book from the bed and noticed the small whiskey bottle sitting on the nightstand.

"Oh...where did you get this?" Higs face lit up. Whiskey and cigarettes had been hard to come by since the war began. Everything was being sent to the men on the frontlines.

"I had to do some serious bartering to get that so don't even think about putting your lips on it."

"Wait until I tell the girls you're holding out on us."

Charley sighed. She knew this was a losing battle. Higs had this persuasive personality and almost always got what she wanted.

"Fine. Go share it with the girls and don't leave the building."

"Yes ma'am." Higs saluted and ran off with the bottle.

Charley smiled and sat back down on the bed with the manual. She waited an hour then decided to go check on her girls. The last thing she needed was them drunk and wandering around the island.

"Hey, Major, come join us. Patterson's just about to deal," Higs said from the makeshift poker table they were gathered around.

"I'm good, thanks," Charley said.

"Here, you can take my spot. These girls are out for blood," one of the women said.

"You girls know this is illegal right?"

Higs shrugged.

"Playing cards is certainly fine, but gambling is against the military code." Charley smiled and sat on the edge of the partial seat offered to her when Higs slid over.

"What are we playing?"

"Straight poker. Fifty-cent buy in," Patterson said, dealing the cards around the table to all six women. A few of the other women were playing Gin at another homemade table, but without all of the seriousness of bluffing and betting that was going on at the poker table.

"You girls are serious," Charley said, flipping two quarters onto the table. She retrieved her chips, tossed in the blind, and picked up her hand. Studying the five cards, she noticed she had a pair of tens, an ace, a three of hearts, and the jack of diamonds.

Four of the women bet and raised the pot a little higher and one folded. Charley looked at her chips. They were basically a penny each and the bet was up to a dime already. She moved a stack of ten chips into the center of the table and called. Everyone turned their cards over and Patterson won the pot with a pair of queens. They gathered up all of the cards and one of the corporals in the squadron began shuffling.

On the next round, Charley checked her cards and anteed up. Everyone made a bet and raised the pot to fifteen-cent. Charley adjusted her chips, met the fifteen-cent, and raised it another two-cent. Higs came behind her and raised it three more cent, making it a full nickel raise for the rest of the table. Everyone folded except Charley who met the three-cent and called.

Higs flipped over three jacks. Charley grinned, turning over each card, one at a time, revealing a flush of clubs.

"Thanks, ladies," Charley said, adding the chips to her stack. She'd managed to win back what she'd lost and double it in one single hand.

The women continued playing for hours. Charley had the largest stack of chips when the radio announced it was midnight.

"Happy New Year everyone. Welcome to 1942," Charley cheered.

***

Valentine's Day was fast approaching and Charley finally got her wish when she saw an Avenger on her log sheet. She walked out of the hangar, looking around at the various planes sitting on the tarmac awaiting her attention. None of them were the Avenger. Just as she was turning to go back inside, she heard the buzz of an incoming plane. It had only been eight weeks since the bombing of Pearl Harbor and every time she'd heard a low flying plane she'd cringed. After arriving on the island, she'd actually run for cover the first few times she'd heard an incoming plane. Since they were on an island in the middle of nowhere surrounded by water is was fairly common for planes to come in low when they were landing, but she couldn't shake the fear she felt when she heard that buzzing sound. Charley spun around to see the Avenger coming towards her with a trail of black smoke on the right side coming from the engine compartment. She watched as the pilot landed the plane and taxied back towards her with the engine spitting and sputtering, threatening to shut off at any moment.

The plane rolled to a stop and the pilot slid down the wing.

"What happened to it?" Charley asked.

"Don't know. We were flying sub patrol missions a few hundred miles from here yesterday and there was a loud bang and then black smoke on the right side. I landed on the carrier and the guys out there took one look at it and the next thing I know I'm being told to bring it to you," the pilot said.

"Alright, let it cool down and I'll take a peek." Charley went back inside the hangar to finish tightening the tail rudder on the Buffalo fighter she'd been working on the previous day.

After lunch, Charley was heading outside to look at the Avenger when Higs stopped her.

"I just got a new letter from Fran," she whispered loudly.

Charley raised an eyebrow. "I didn't know you two kept in touch."

"Yes, we write every week or so. She told me she and Audrey have been assigned to the USHS *Solace*. It's a Navy hospital ship. They are staying in the Pacific for now."

"I wish them all the best. Now, if you will excuse me I have a lovely grey lady waiting on the tarmac for my services." Charley walked away as if hearing Audrey's name meant nothing to her.

Charley placed the ladder next to the Avenger, climbed up, and popped open the right side engine compartment door. The air reeked with the rancid smell of burnt oil. The entire right side of the engine was covered in a sticky black substance that she knew was oil and grit mixed together. She climbed back down the ladder and went into the hangar. She returned to the plane a few minutes later with a spray can and rags. She sprayed the cleaner and used the rags to wipe away as much of the greasy oil as possible. She finally found what she'd thought she would see when she wiped the side of the engine block next to the header. The header gasket had a small tear on the top. It wasn't exactly the easiest repair job, but it was one she was familiar with. She climbed down the ladder and pulled the Avenger into the hangar with the tractor tug. When she had the bomber parked where she wanted it she chocked the tires and moved the ladder back to the same position at the open engine compartment.

"Oh, this is different. Wait, is this that new Avenger bomber from the carriers?" Patterson asked.

"Sure is," Charley said.

"What's wrong with it?"

"Blown header gasket."

Charley grabbed the couple of socket wrenches she was going to need and headed up the ladder.

"You almost done changing the oil in that Wildcat?" Charley asked.

"Yes, ma'am."

"Good. There's a Vindicator from the same carrier outside that I believe has a bent tail wheel. Check the log first." Charley went to work loosening bolts to the pieces she needed to remove in order to get the header off the side of the engine.

Chapter Eleven

"Major," Higs said, knocking on her door. It was St. Patrick's Day and the girls were all dressed in their uniforms and going over to the mess hall to drink green beer and celebrate with the other aircrews and sailors. Charley didn't feel much like going.

"Go have a good time, Higs. You can tell me all about it tomorrow."

"Well, if you don't want this letter that came in the mail for you, then I guess I will have to read it," Higs teased.

Charley flung the door open. "What letter?"

"This one." Higs stuck the envelope in her face. Charley snatched it and closed the door.

Charley read the outside of the envelope and raised an eyebrow. She waited until the footsteps and noise in the hallway were gone, before tearing it open as she sat down on her bed.

Dear Charley,

I'm not sure if you are going to even read this or not, but I know Fran has been writing letters back and forth with SSgt. Higginbotham. I don't know if you even know that. Anyway, I've been assigned to a Navy hospital ship called the USHS *Solace.* I'm not exactly happy about it. I've never been partial to sea travel. My grandparents perished on the *Titanic* leaving my mother and her sister orphaned. They wound up living with a distant relative, but life was never the same for them.

The ship is an old passenger ship that was converted last year. We are assigned to the Pacific and have been down around New Guinea. I've seen some of the most beautiful places. It's hard to believe they are in the middle of a war zone. We're on our way now closer to New Zealand over the next few weeks. Then, back to Pearl Harbor or San Francisco. We've been stopping in ports to tend to the wounded and moving on.

Life is definitely much different than being on Ford Island. We sleep in racks, four to a room, and the bathroom situation isn't exactly female friendly. I miss the sunrises and sunsets. I spend my days in the belly of the ship only feeling the sun on my face occasionally.

I hope you are well. Fran tells me Higs has written a lot about the island you are on and best describes it as roughing it like you're all camping. Hopefully, you won't be stationed there much longer. I should probably get this letter out since we are leaving port in the morning. Please take care of yourself. I miss you.

Yours Always,

Audrey

PS

That pilot that you were looking for, Lt. Davis, was sent back stateside. He had to have both legs amputated. I didn't know if you ever found him or not before you left.

Charley folded the letter neatly, placing it back in the envelope. She stood up and walked to her door then back to the bed. The envelope seemed to be staring up watching her every move as she paced in her bare feet on the cool concrete floor. Running a hand through her hair, she took a deep breath, sat back down on the bed, and opened the envelope again. She studied the feminine curves of the loopy handwriting as her chest tightened. This was the last thing she needed. She didn't want contact on purpose. She didn't want to be reminded, not of the bombing, the deaths, or the magical feeling of falling in love with a beautiful woman. Being in the middle of a war wasn't all sunshine and roses and writing a letter pretending it was just wasn't worth her time. Charley balled the letter up and tossed it in the box in the corner that doubled as a wastebasket, and reached for the bottle under her mattress.

The golden liquid sloshed in the bottle of whiskey Charley had traded her watch for as she pressed it to her lips and tipped it up. She never cared for the watch to begin with and time seemed to move at a snail's pace since she'd arrived on Midway. A small glass bottle of cheap whiskey was well worth the trade. Charley drank a few long swigs from the bottle and put the cork back in it. Swinging her legs up on the bed, she leaned back against the wall.

"Happy St. Patty's Day," she said to the empty room.

***

"Good morning, Major," Patterson said cheerfully, walking past her in the hangar.

"What's so good about it?" Charley asked from her position in the cockpit of a Wildcat fighter.

"The sun's shining, we're ahead of schedule, and no one's dropping bombs on our heads. It is a good day." Higs stuck her head out from under the wing of the plane Charley was sitting in. Patterson kept walking towards the Buffalo fighter awaiting her attention on the other side of the packed hangar.

Charley shook her head and went back to tightening the new oil lines in the cockpit. In a way, Higs did have a point. They were constantly hearing about the battle on the frontlines as the war progressed and she was generally happy the Japs decided not to return.

"So," Higs said.

"So what?" Charley lifted her head, waiting for a response.

"What did it say?"

"What did what say?"

"The letter," Higs huffed. Charley had a feeling that if Higs had feathers like a chicken they would definitely be ruffled at the moment.

"To tell you what it said would imply that I read it," Charley stated simply and went back to what she was doing.

"You didn't read it?" Higs' voice rose high enough to produce a squeak.

Charley rolled her eyes and poked her head out of the cockpit.

"Whether or not I read it and what it may or may not have said is none of your business. Get back to work. I'm almost done here and I plan to push this plane out within the next twenty-minutes."

"Fran says they are doing well, but hate being assigned to that stinky old ship. She said it's like being closed up in a tin can that's baking in the oven."

"I don't care what Audrey is doing."

Higs ignored her. "At least we get fresh air every day. I'm claustrophobic. I'd die on a Navy ship."

Charley dropped a wrench over the side of the fuselage that landed close to where Higs was working replacing loose rivets.

"Hey, you almost hit me!"

"You nit wit. You climb into the tight engine compartments, cockpits, and cargo holds all day. You're not claustrophobic."

"I'm not in them for days on end with no sunlight or fresh air."

Charley climbed out of the cockpit and slid down the wing. "I'm ready to fire up this bird and check these new lines. Are you done flapping your gums?"

"I have two rivets to change out and she's all yours," Higs said.

Charley hopped up on the tractor and waited for Higs to finish her work. When she'd finished she hooked the landing gear to the tractor and Charley pushed the small fighter out of the hangar, lining it up next to the other finished planes on the tarmac. Midway Island was so overrun with planes they were almost sitting on top of each other in perfect rows down each runway.

Charley jumped off the tractor and chocked the plane's wheels. Higs jumped on the tractor to go pull another plane inside as Charley climbed into the Wildcat cockpit. She choked the engine, opened the throttle, and pushed the button to begin spinning the prop of the rotary engine. The plane quickly coughed and sputtered as it came to life. Charley watched the oil pressure gauge and checked the new lines for leaks in the cramped space. She tested the hydraulics, moving the foot pedals back and forth. Satisfied that everything was working correctly, she shut the plane down and climbed out.

"Pass the test?" Higs asked when she saw Charley walking towards the closet-sized room with a window that doubled as her office.

"Can't get any better than perfect," she said, grabbing the clipboard with the log sheet.

Chapter Twelve

Charley's rickety bed creaked when she sat up and stretched. The sun was close to rising over the island and she needed to hurry if she wanted to catch the sunrise services. She wasn't much of a church person, believing everyone made their own choices no matter what the church's influence were. Still, she never missed Easter Sunrise Service. She quickly donned her drab green WAAC Dress Uniform and garrison cap.

When she stepped out of her room it was quiet, too quiet, which meant she'd obviously missed her squad and more than likely her ride in the yard truck that came by for them. She closed the door to the barracks building and began walking towards the old storage building that had been turned into a church on the other side of the island. The service was being held outside on the one and only patch of grass found on the island that happened to be next to the church.

Charley barely heard a noise on the gravel before she was clobbered from behind and knocked flat on her face.

"Son of a bitch," she yelled and spit dirt from her mouth as she stood up. Her uniform was covered in a

91

light white and grey powder from the gravel path she was walking on.

"I'm so sorry, ma'am. I didn't see you."

Charley spun around, facing the young sailor lying on the ground. The tires on the bicycle next to him were still spinning. She shook her head in disgust and began brushing the dirt from her pants and jacket. He jumped to his feet, saluting her when he saw the gold leaf on her collar.

"Are you headed to Sunrise Service?" he asked when she returned the salute.

"No, I'm meeting the General for breakfast, you nit wit. Yes, I'm going to service."

"You're a little late," he said, gathering his bicycle from the dirt.

"Thanks to you I'm a lot late. Now, get your pansy ass out of my way before I have you tossed in the brig for assaulting an officer," Charley growled as she began walking away.

"Can I give you a ride? I really am sorry."

Charley looked at the bright colors beginning to appear on the horizon. She spun around, raising an eyebrow. "Are you offering me your bike?"

"No, ma'am. I'm offering you a ride on the handlebars."

"What the hell? The handlebars? Are you trying to kill me?"

He poked his small chest out. "I'm a good driver. I honestly didn't see you in the dark. You're going to miss the service unless you hop on."

Charley walked over to where he was. Standing ramrod straight, she stared into his beady little eyes. "You dump me off or crash with me on here and I will make sure you get put on agriculture duty, shoveling animal shit in the middle of Texas. Do you understand me?"

"Yes, ma'am," he said.

Charley reluctantly climbed up onto the thin rail of the handlebars, gripping it for dear-life with both hands. The young sailor pedaled away from the scene of their accident, gaining speed quickly and bouncing them all over the gravel path.

"Slow down," Charley yelled.

"You want to get there in time for the start of service don't you?"

Charley gritted her teeth. Her knuckles were white and burning from her grasp on the thin bar under her butt.

A few minutes later, they skidded to a stop near the church. Charley jumped down, wiping the rest of the loose dirt from her uniform as she walked towards the rows of chairs on the other side of the building.

"I was wondering if you were going to make it," Higs said as Charley slid into the seat next to her.

"I slept in."

"What the hell happened to you?" Higs asked when she noticed the frumpy condition of Charley's usually pressed and fitted uniform.

"Don't ask," Charley whispered as the clergyman stepped to the front of the group and began his sermon with a short hymn. The orange and red hues of the rising sun lit up the sky in multiple rays behind him.

Charley opened the hymnal that she'd removed from her seat, opened it to the correct hymn, and began singing along with everyone around her.

When the service ended, Charley was walking towards the yard truck with most of her squad when the young man came by, pedaling his bicycle around the small group.

"Major," he said and saluted.

"Seaman." Charley nodded, returning the salute.

"How do you know him? And what happened to your clothes?" Patterson raised an eyebrow.

"Mind your own business, Corporal," said Charley. Walking past her, she climbed into the front seat of the yard truck. With the morning she'd had she wasn't in the mood to ride in the back with the others.

***

A few weeks later, Charley was just finishing her shower and wishing there was a tub to soak in when the cheap flap the women used as a makeshift shower curtain flew open. Charley grabbed the other side of the thin flap pulling it haphazardly across her body.

"What the hell?" she yelled.

"There you are. I've been looking all over for you," Higs panted.

"What is so damn important?"

"You got another letter." Higs held the envelope up in the air.

"Oh, good grief, Higs. Get out of my damn shower before I demote you!" Charley said, snatching the curtain and turning her back.

She'd already had a rough day. She had been covered in hydraulic oil when the line she'd just repaired burst under pressure, spraying her from head to toe. She'd washed her hair three times and still couldn't get the stinky, sticky mess out of it. It didn't help that she'd also twisted her back trying to get the spray under control so she could cap the line. She just wanted to go lie on her stiff as a board mattress and pray for sleep to claim her. Reading a reminder letter was the last thing on her mind.

Charley washed her hair for the fourth time and gave up on it ever being clean again. She noticed the letter when she reached for her towel. Pushing it to the side, she toweled off and quickly dressed. At the last minute, she stuffed the letter into her pocket.

Returning to her room, Charley hung her towel on the rod behind the door and put her toiletry kit in her foot locker. She forgot all about the letter until she felt it crinkle when she sat on the bed. She pulled it out and read the return address. Audrey was obviously still on the *Solace*. Charley wadded the envelope into a ball, tossed it into the trash box, and turned off the dim overhead light.

She finally fell asleep after tossing and turning on the scratchy sheet most of the night. She wasn't ready to get up, but the bugler playing the morning colors outside reminded her that she had a job to do so she sat up and stretched her sore back.

***

"I posted a letter this morning to Nurse Sutton," said Higs.

"Oh really." Charley wasn't paying much attention to the Staff Sergeant as she talked her ear off the entire morning. She tuned Higs out when she began talking about Fran and Audrey and their adventures on the high seas in the tin can. She regretted scheduling Higs to help her replace the tail hook on the Avenger, but none of the other women had ever performed that type of repair so she figured she would teach Higs and let her pass it along. Teaching and training was by all means a big part of being a Staff Sergeant anyway, as well as leadership.

"Did you hear anything I just said to you?"

"Yes, you mentioned something about posting a letter to Fran," Charley said, collecting her tools from the floor. They were finally finished.

"Not Fran. I said Nurse Sutton."

"Oh."

"I want to know how to remove the stick you have up your butt," Higs huffed.

Charley was taken aback for a second. She just stood there staring at Higs before she began to laugh hysterically.

"What's so funny?" asked Higs.

"I was picturing her face as she read it."

"Well, with the way you've been acting lately maybe I really should post it."

"I'm not sorry, Higs. I've said before that I don't want to be hounded. The thing between Audrey and me is my personal business and whatever it was, it's over. I don't want to talk about it or about her."

"I won't bring it up again, Major," Higs said.

"Thank you. Now, can we get back to work? We have a Dauntless and two Marauders that need oil changes. Take your pick. I want all of them finished by the end of the week."

"I'll do all three if you come out of your room and play cards with us tonight. I need to win my money back."

Charley thought about it for a minute and nodded her head. She was always hesitant spending time with her girls outside of the hangar, except for Higs and Patterson, but a little illegal game of poker would be harmless.

When Charley walked into their barracks building, the girls already had the poker table set up and were waiting impatiently for her arrival. She'd stayed a little later to update the log sheets and had lost track of time. Luckily, she had been able to flag down a yard truck in the dark to catch a ride back to her building.

"Let me go clean up and change my clothes. Leave me a seat open next to Patterson. I know she doesn't cheat," Charley said with a smile as she headed towards the stairs.

After an hour of play, Charley had a stack of chips twice as large as anyone else at the table. She hated taking their money, but she couldn't help it.

"I can't believe it's May already," said Patterson.

"I know, one more month to go." one of the other girls said.

"What are your plans for leave, Major?" Higs asked.

Charley hadn't really thought much about their upcoming week of leave. Since they were stationed on an island away from any type of civilian life where they could have leave or liberty weekends, they were granted a week of leave in three different stages so as they weren't all gone at the same time. The first stage was scheduled for the second week of June and then the two subsequent weeks. Most of the girls had plans to go home and see their families.

"I'm not sure yet," Charley said.

Chapter Thirteen

It was the middle of May and Charley still hadn't decided what she wanted to do on her week of leave. She was sitting on the jetty rocks with a homemade fishing pole that she'd constructed out of a long stick, a piece of string, and a hook she'd made out of a piece of chicken pen wire. She'd spent every day off sitting on this rock fishing since the week she arrived on Midway.

She felt the stick in her hands move slightly. She jerked quickly, and began pulling the string up to reveal the small fish flopping on the end. She took it off the hook gently and smiled as she put the fish back in the water to live another day. She thought of going home. She wanted to see her mother, but then she'd spend a week listening to why she didn't need to be a part of this war. That was out of the question and being an only child she didn't have brothers and sisters to go visit, which of course had made things worse for her mother when she'd found out she couldn't have any more children. Charley sometimes wished she did have someone special in her life to share her leave with.

"Is this considered a form of entertainment?" Patterson asked, sitting down next to Charley on the large rock.

"It is if you're me," Charley said.

"I always see you out here when we're you're off schedule. Do you catch anything?"

"Just caught a sea trout."

"Where is it?" Patterson looked around the rocks.

Charley pointed down at the water and Patterson raised an eyebrow.

"I threw it back. I don't keep them."

"Oh. I thought fishermen kept their catch?"

"Well, yeah if you're going to cook it or sell it. I fish because it's peaceful and I enjoy it."

"Maybe you should sell the next one to the mess hall. That chow they served for lunch today was unidentifiable."

Charley laughed. She knew the Navy supply ship hadn't come in as scheduled the week before and the entire base was up in arms as to what to do about it. The commissary shelves were empty and the mess hall was obviously running very low on key ingredients. Cigarettes were a very hot commodity and many of the sailors and airmen would trade just about anything or pay just about anything to get their hands on some smokes. Charley used this time to barter her way to another bottle of whiskey, a small radio for her room, and a few other things, as well as a free haircut that she was in dire need of. She hated her hair being long at all and military regulations said it couldn't touch her collar so she kept it as short as femininely possibly. Trying to put bobby pins in her curly hair was like tying knots around sticks and trying to get them out. The first time she'd pinned her hair back she'd had to cut more than half of the pins out.

"So you think I can make some money off my fish, huh?"

"Yes, ma'am and I'd much rather eat fresh fish than some kind of canned sloppy substance that closely resembles dog food."

Charley was about to say something when the stick moved again. She jerked back and began pulling up the string. Patterson watched in amazement as the fish broke the surface, wiggling all around.

"Wow," Patterson said with her eyes as big as saucers. She watched Charley release the fish from the hook and set it back in the water where it swam off. "Why didn't you keep it?"

"Do you know how many people are stationed on this base?" Charley asked.

"I don't know."

"Both islands together probably have a few thousand sailors and airmen. Do you know how many fish I would need to catch to feed everyone?"

"I guess you're right," Patterson said disappointingly.

"I'll tell you what," Charley said, putting the line back in the water. "You go find the rest of our squadron and see who likes fish. I saw an old fire pit when I was walking the beach on the other side of the island behind the PBY yard. If I can get into the mess hall kitchen to get some supplies, I'll make fish dinner for you girls tonight."

"Yes!" Patterson jumped up from her sitting position almost falling head first into the water on the slippery rock.

"Tell Higs to get off her ass and come out here. I know she's probably reading or writing a letter."

"She and a few of the other girls are on the beach tossing a pie pan back and forth with some sailors."

Charley cocked her head to the side.

Patterson shrugged. "I don't know. One of the guys said it was popular where he was from."

"I see. Well, go tell her I need her assistance on a code black project."

"Yes, ma'am."

"Oh and Patterson, have you ever cleaned a fish?"

"No."

"Well, you're going to learn," Charley grinned and leaned back against the jetty.

***

A few hours later, Higs walked into the hangar and slammed the door shut. Patterson was standing by the tool bench with Charley.

"I got everything you asked for. It cost me a carton and a half of smokes," said Higs.

"Damn swabbies," Charley said, taking the old milk crate from Higs. She pulled out a cast iron frying pan, a metal pot, a sharp knife, a long fork, a bag of rice, and various jars of seasoning.

"Higs, help Patterson carry the pliers and those boards over there. We're going out behind the hangar."

"She's going to teach us how to clean fish," Patterson exclaimed.

Higs raised an eyebrow. "Patterson, have you ever seen a fish get cleaned?"

"Nope."

"Do you know what happens when you clean a fish?"

"Nope."

"Oh leave her alone. You're cleaning them too. I have to go get that fire pit going," said Charley.

The three women walked behind the hangar where Charley had the pile of fish sitting in the shade on an old board. She took the first fish and laid it out by itself, taking the large knife from the crate she chopped it's head off in one swift motion, and began slicing the skin back.

"Oh my god!" Patterson put her hand over her mouth.

Higs shook her head and rolled her eyes. Patterson was so naive it was almost comical. Then again, in 1942 it wasn't common for a woman to go fishing or know how to clean a fish.

"Okay, did you see how I peeled the layers back until I found the bones? You flip it over and do the same thing on the other side. Then, just cut the tail off and you have all of the layers of meat. This is called filleting. It shouldn't take you guys too long. When you're done, wrap it all up in the newspaper and bring it to me. You'll see the smoke from the fire on the other side of the PBY landing by the yard." Charley took off towards the other side of the island with the rest of the wood and a piece of newspaper in the crate, along with the utensils, and a pocket full of matches.

***

Charley had the fire going nicely with a pot of water heating on one side when the women appeared with the newspaper full of fish fillets. The rest of the group that had wanted a fish dinner were spread out on the beach near the water. She opened the paper, took the fillets out, and lapped them on both sides with the lemon butter mixture, and placed them on the grate that she had fashioned out of scrap metal. She sprinkled salt and pepper and a few other spices on the fish and flipped them over to repeat the sprinkle of spices. She poured the rice into the boiling water and tossed some spices in with it. A few minutes later, she took the pot off the fire and flipped the fish. When everything was finished, she fixed each person a plate of rice with two fish fillets.

"Damn, this is really good. Who knew you could cook, Major. What other talents are you hiding from us?" Higs teased.

Charley rolled her eyes and grinned behind a bite of food.

All of the girls sang her praises as they cleared their plates and peered at the fire casually looking for more fish.

"No more fish, ladies, sorry. But, I do have dessert for everyone that runs down to the water to wash their dishes," Charley said. Most of the group jumped up and took off towards the water.

Charley took the dozen sticks she'd found on the beach and in the dunes and placed a marshmallow on the end of each one and handed them to the girls as they returned. She opened the handful of chocolate bars and graham crackers she brought from her stash in her room and showed everyone how to hold their marshmallow in the fire until it was flaming. She explained how to put everything together to make some-mores.

"Now I'm really curious about your talents," Higs said between bites. "Where in the world did you learn to make these? And how the hell did you score chocolate?"

Charley laughed. "My dad was an Army soldier in World War One. He loved camping and took me with him often. He taught me everything he knew up until the war took his life," Charley said casually. "As for the chocolate you'd be surprised what those dumbass swabbies will trade for smokes and trust me the ones on the ships have much more to offer than the ones stationed here."

"Our Major, the swindler, who knew?" Higs laughed.

"We're at war and inflation is high. What can I say?" Charley shrugged and laughed.

When they'd finished the bag of marshmallows, Charley poured water and sand on the fire pit and began stuffing the materials back into the crate.

"What time did you say you'd have these utensils back?" she asked Higs.

"Tomorrow morning."

"Good, you're in charge of making sure they're returned. Everyone else, have a good evening. I will see you all in the morning," Charley said.

The group stood and saluted their outstanding Squadron CO. She smiled and saluted in return before heading back across the island.

Chapter Fourteen

June had barely arrived, bringing the searing heat right along with it. The cool breeze blowing over the island couldn't compete with the hot rays of the sun. As summer approached, Charley's squadron found themselves spending more time repairing or replacing rusty parts than anything else. The sticky salt air clung to everything this time of year and it was hell on airplane metal.

"I think it's hotter here than Pearl." Higs wiped the sweat from her brow with a rag.

Charley shrugged.

"I'm beginning to think the Navy dips their planes in saltwater."

Charley laughed, "Why is that?"

"All of this damn rust! For the past two days all I've been doing is cleaning rust from props, wings, landing gears, and anything else it wants to corrode. These planes are covered in rust and they're supposed to be back on their carrier this afternoon because they are leaving for some patrol mission or something," Higs huffed.

"Go pull a few of the girls off the trucks to help you. Those oil changes on the yard trucks can wait. These planes need to be top priority."

***

Charley was having trouble sleeping and had just dozed off when the base scramble siren rang out loudly at midnight. Charley jumped out of bed and quickly dressed in her daily drab green work uniform and gathered her squadron.

"This isn't a drill, ladies. Take cover and keep an eye on the skies," she said, ushering them out the door to wait for the yard truck.

Charley climbed into the front seat of the truck. The whining of the siren pierced her ears.

"Are we under attack?" she asked the young seaman driving quickly across the base.

"Damn Japs just bombed Dutch Harbor."

The truck careened to a stop and took off again once everyone was out. The women swung the heavy hangar doors open and watched the dark skies as Charley ran into her tiny office to grab the ringing phone from her desk.

"Major, your orders are to help ready as many planes as you can. This is not a drill. The Japs are close by and we need all of our birds in the air."

Charley stared at the phone when she heard the dial tone. This couldn't possibly be happening again. She slammed the phone down, walked out into the hangar, and climbed up on a scaffold ladder.

"Attention," she yelled.

All of the women in the squadron popped to attention standing ramrod straight.

"We need to take a look at all of the planes on our log and begin fueling and pushing back the ones that are flyable. If the plane is awaiting an oil change, fuel it and push it back. If it's a simple rust or corrosion repair, fuel it and push it back. The pilots will be arriving shortly so let's have planes ready for them, ladies." Charley climbed halfway down before she was stopped by questions.

"The Japs just attacked another island and are in our area. We could be under attack very shortly and we need to be ready. Keep your eyes on the skies and stay away from anything that will fall on your head or explode next to you."

Charley jumped off the bottom of the ladder and began scrolling through the log of planes on the clipboard in her hand.

"How far away are the planes?" Higs asked quietly.

"I don't think they know. That's why they are readying all of the planes to begin patrolling for them."

"Oh my god, it's Pearl all over again."

"Let's hope not," Charley said, walking towards the open hangar doors. The girls had already begun tagging planes with red ribbon for the ones that weren't flight ready. The rest were being fueled two at a time.

They had sixteen planes on the log and from the looks of it at least six of them would be able to fly immediately. Charley and Higs began pushing planes back and starting them just as a small group of pilots arrived in the yard truck.

"We have four birds on the line now and two more coming behind them," she yelled to the pilots.

Charley pulled the chocks away and watched each plane roll towards the runway. Once the planes were gone, the entire squadron stood outside of the hangar near the line watching the quiet blackened skies.

Two hours later, the girls were working faster than ever before. They were outside doing minimal repairs on the other handful of planes that were close to being flight ready and drinking coffee while waiting for the sun to hurry up and rise. Their planes had returned for refueling with no signs of the enemy carriers or planes and the other planes in the fleet had returned at various times with the same result.

"Are we sure they're even out there?" one of the girls said.

"If the base CO says they are then they are. It's just a matter of finding them before they find us," Charley said, tightening the last bolt on the new prop she'd just put on a dauntless bomber. They had all but four of their planes flight ready. The last four were in pieces and awaiting parts or major repairs.

At four-thirty a.m., the sun began coming up. They watched a group of Navy PBY planes take off from the water on the other side of the island and almost directly in front of them a half dozen B-17 fortress bombers took off from the Army Air Force fleet.

At five-forty-five a.m., the siren wailed again. Charley rushed inside the hangar to wait for the phone. A minute later, it rang. She picked it up, hearing the words she'd been dreading to hear.

"Listen up ladies, this is it. That was the scramble order. Enemy planes have been spotted. We need to get all of the planes on the line and in the air now!" she yelled.

Twenty minutes later, the last of the planes got off the ground and Japanese Kate dive bombers and Zero fighters came in behind them, dropping bombs and strafing the island.

"Get out of the hangar!" Charley screamed and dove for cover under a nearby tool cart.

Bombs exploded all around causing the small island to literally shutter. Strafing bullets riddled the ground a few feet from Charley's position. Thick black smoke filled the air from the fires of the PBY seaplane hangar and all three oil tanks exploded. Charley climbed out from under the tool cart and looked around. The buildings around the airbase were still standing including her hangar and the airstrips were strafed, but still useable. Many buildings in the distance were smoking from fires or destroyed and others were damaged. Multiple planes were strafed with bullet holes and a few were mangled from exploding bombs.

The smell of the burning oil sent Charley's mind right back to Pearl Harbor. When the buzzing of the planes and gunfire moved into the distance, she gathered her squadron to get an injury report and surprisingly there were only cuts, scrapes, and bruises. No one had been seriously hurt.

"That was twenty minutes of hell," Higs wrapped a rag around the shrapnel cut on her arm.

"It looks like everything is intact. That Marauder over there is toast." She pointed to the plane that was badly strafed with one wing barely attached. "The hangar was barely hit though," Charley said.

"It looks like the Buffalos had their layers peeled back," Higs pointed to the two mangled pieces of metal that were once fighter planes.

"Dive bombers," Charley said, shaking her head.

"Incoming!" Patterson shouted, pointing to the skies.

The low buzzing of incoming planes sent everyone scrambling for cover once again as a small group of the base planes landed for refueling. Charley realized these planes were landing and quickly readied her squadron to go to work refueling them and assessing damage before sending them back into the air.

"Where is the rest of the base fleet?" Charley asked one of the pilots whose plane was shot up and had barely made it back to the base.

"In the drink. They shot half of us down within minutes," he said, shaking his head. "Most of the carrier planes are still in the air giving them hell though."

"At least we were ready for them this time," Charley said. She had just finished assessing the damage on his plane and was about to patch the oil leak and send him back up when another air strike strafed the island. She and the pilot dove to the ground rolling away from the damaged plane together as it exploded.

The small wave of planes disappeared quickly. Charley jumped to her feet looking all around the sky for more planes.

"Son of a bitch!" she yelled.

"I need to get back up there. What have you got that flies, Major?" the pilot said, watching the skies as well.

"Nothing. Well, I do have a Wildcat fighter awaiting repairs. It's in the hangar."

Charley ran towards the hangar with the pilot.

"What's wrong with it?" he asked.

"The hydraulics for the landing gear are broken and it's leaking oil. It'll get you up, but more than likely it won't last long and probably won't hold your landing."

"Get it on the line," he said, pushing other equipment out of the way so the plane could be moved.

Charley brought the fuel truck over and began fueling the plane after Higs used the tractor to pull the plane outside.

"Fly safe," Charley said, to him as he climbed up into the cockpit. She backed away and watched him roll down the taxiway towards the runway.

"Doesn't that plane have a broken landing gear and an oil leak?" Patterson asked.

"Yes."

"Do you think they're coming back?" one of Charley's squad members said, looking towards the sky. The oil tanks were still burning flames with thick black smoke billowing overhead.

"I hope not," Charley stated and went back to assessing the damage around them.

The service squadron spent the rest of the day refueling and adding oil to the limited planes coming back to the base. Most of them had strafing marks and oil leaks, but they were going right back up to fight again. So far, the Wildcat's landing gear had held. Charley had seen that same plane land and take back off a couple of times during the long day. The Japanese made no more appearances over the island.

Chapter Fifteen

The base planes flew missions throughout the night and most of the next day, chasing the Japanese planes away from the island and bombing their fleet of carriers. They'd managed to sink two of the Japanese carriers.

Charley's squadron was climbing out of the yard truck close to the hangar the following morning when she noticed a plane coming in low over the runway, spitting and sputtering. It was the Wildcat fighter she knew all too well. Obviously, the oil leak had gotten worse sometime during the night. She watched as the landing gear deployed and the pilot touched down. The tail was barely down when the landing gear collapsed, pushing the plane onto its belly. The plane skidded across the runway and flipped on its side as it came to a stop.

Charley jumped back in the cab of the truck.

"Get to that plane!" she yelled. The driver stomped the gas pedal in the heavy old truck just as the plane exploded in a ball of flames.

When the truck came to a stop a hundred yards away from the burning wreckage, Charley dove out barely connecting with the ground before she began running

112

towards the pilot laying on the ground thirty feet from the flames. She slid to stop, bending down next to him.

"Did you see that landing?" he coughed and grinned. "I guess you were right."

Charley helped him to his feet. "You've got some balls. I knew it would happen sooner or later. I kept watching you land all day yesterday thinking this has to be it."

"It would've been fine if the damn thing didn't toss itself at the end there. I was out and walking away when the explosion sent me flying through the air."

"You've got guts, I'll give you that. Hell, all you pilots are crazy out there flying broken and battered planes." Charley shook her head.

"I shot down three of those sons-of-bitches in that tin can full of holes with no landing gear!" He smiled and lit a smoke.

Charley nodded towards the cigarette pack and he handed her one. She hadn't smoked in close to three years, but her stress level couldn't get much higher, so she lit it and took a long drag. She coughed and wheezed, took another feel good drag, and climbed into the back of the truck with the pilot.

"What's your name, Major?"

"Charley. You?"

"Robert," he said, sticking his hand out. "I guess I should be saluting you."

Charley smiled. "I'll let it slide this time. I should probably be the one saluting you. If it wasn't for you guys up in the air this base would be in a lot worse shape than it is."

"I wasn't at Pearl, but I heard it was pretty bad."

"There was no air. The skies were so thick with heavy black smoke and soot from Battleship Row that you couldn't see anything and your lungs burned. Most of the buildings were either collapsed or on fire or both. The men in the water were screaming so loud you could hear them all over the island. It was worse than hell itself." Charley took the last drag from her smoke and flicked it out the back of the truck.

"Wow. So, you were there?"

"Yes. My squadron was stationed on Ford Island. We lost one of our members when the hangar she was in collapsed and exploded from a dive bomb," Charley said.

The pilot leaned over and offered her another smoke just as the truck pulled up outside of the hangar. Charley took it and smiled.

"I'll see you around, Robert."

Charley stood outside of the hangar smoking and watching the planes flying overhead. The US forces continued patrolling the skies until they knew for sure that the enemy was gone. She personally hoped they'd sunk every one of their damn ships.

"Here you are. I've been looking all over for you. Since when do you smoke? Give me that thing," Higs said, taking a drag from the cigarette.

"It takes the wonders of war to make a retired smoker smoke again," Charley sighed and put the cigarette out when Higs handed it back to her. "What's so important?"

"I saw that plane go down. Was that our Wildcat?"

"Yeah, the pilot is fine though. He shot down three enemy planes in that piece of shit plane until it gave out on him."

"Way to go, crazy pilot."

"I heard from the yard truck driver that the latest report is only three or four casualties on the island. Everyone did a hell of a job getting the entire fleet into the air."

"That's good. I think we lost over a hundred planes from our base and the ships total. I heard someone talking about it last night."

"Wow. I heard something about a Navy carrier and destroyer. We must have lost them too."

"It still wasn't as bad as it could've been," Higs said, adjusting the bandage covering the cut on her arm.

"We're all alive. That's what matters to me. Come on, we have a pile of planes to fix."

Chapter Sixteen

A few days later, the USHS *Solace* docked in Midway. Many of the nurses went ashore to assess the injuries and restock the dispensary with much needed medical equipment.

Charley had no idea the ship was coming or had arrived. She was busy replacing a strafed wing panel on an Avenger when she heard a soft voice and spun around almost causing the loose wing to fall on her head.

"Careful there, Major. I wouldn't want you to bump your head again on my account," Audrey smiled shyly.

"Uh...hi...what..." Charley cleared her throat and walked Audrey towards her office.

"I know you don't want to see me. I just had to know you were okay," Audrey said.

"I'm as okay as I can be, I guess."

"My heart dropped when we heard the news. I kept praying you were alright."

"We have a lot of destruction and some injuries, but there weren't many casualties and thankfully, all of my girls are fine," Charley leaned against the small desk.

"That's good to hear. I'm glad you're not hurt. Can I see you later? Tonight, maybe?"

116

"Audrey,"

"Please, Charley. I just want to talk to you. I don't know when I will ever see you again."

"Okay. There are large dunes close to the jetty on the other side of the island near the destroyed seaplane hangar. We are restricted to lights out at dark incase those bastards come back. If I'm not there when you get there, I'll meet you just after lights out."

Charley let Audrey out of her office and watched her walk away. She sighed and turned back towards the plane she was working on.

"That didn't look like it went well," Higs said.

Charley raised an eyebrow. "What's that supposed to mean?"

"I know you haven't returned any of her letters."

"Is that all you and Fran write about in your three page letters?" Charley growled.

"Well no, but..."

"Then stay out of my business. When I want you in it, I will invite you. Until then, we have work to do," Charley ran her hand through her hair and put her cap back on. "Besides, I'm seeing her tonight after lights out," she whispered.

Higs smiled and nodded.

***

Lights out had come and gone and Charley was sitting alone in the dunes smoking a cigarette, watching the oil tanks burning brightly in the dark night sky. There was no sign of Audrey and she wondered if maybe she was caught or unable to get away.

"Sorry I'm late," Audrey whispered from a few feet away.

"I waited."

"I didn't know you smoked," Audrey said surprisingly, sitting down next to Charley on the piece of wood between the dunes.

"I quit a few years ago, but I've been through hell twice in six months with bombs dropping on my head, so if I feel like having a smoke I think I've damn well earned the right." Charley took the last drag and buried the fire in the sand.

"I can't argue with that. I'm really glad you're okay. I hear you make a mean sea trout."

Charley grinned. "It's better than the shit they've been feeding us."

"I hope you're not stationed here much longer. I've been so worried about you."

"That's why I didn't want to start anything in the first place, Audrey. We're at war and war is unpredictable. I don't want to constantly be wondering where you are and if you're okay when I hear about attacks. Plus, I seem to have a target on my ass for the Japanese. If something were to happen to me it wouldn't be fair to you."

"I can't help it, Charley. I'm in love with you," Audrey wiped a tear from her cheek.

Charley wrapped her arms around Audrey. Holding her tenderly, she kissed the top of her head and tucked it under her chin.

"I'd be lying to you if I said I didn't love you too. I just don't know how to do this, Audrey."

"We'll do it together," said Audrey, wrapping her arms tightly around Charley's waist.

"It's not that easy."

"I never said it would be easy, Charley." Audrey pulled back enough to look at Charley's eyes in the soft moonlight. "I'm not that naive young nurse you met the day you cut your head. I've changed. The things I've seen and done..." Audrey shook her head. "War changes people."

Charley sighed. "You're telling me. I don't think I even remember the person I was before I joined the service, not to mention going through two attacks. So much so, that I was scared to go home on my leave. It doesn't matter now, I'm sure that's been canceled since we just got blown to bits again."

"I think you're an amazing person, Charley. Those women in your squadron have been to hell and back with you and they would do it all over again tomorrow because of the leader that you are."

"That's all I know how to do." Charley waved her hand between them. "This...I have no idea how to do this."

Audrey smiled and kissed her lips.

"That's what I love about you. You're this iron-willed person and by-the-book leader, but with me you're vulnerable and sincere. Beneath that hard shell exterior lays an incredible woman."

Charley smiled. "You think you know me so well."

"Am I wrong?"

Charley shook her head.

"Charley, there are no promises. There can't be, not like this, not in the middle of a war that is pulling us in different directions. I just want to know you're out there somewhere and wherever you are you miss me and love me as much as I do you. That's all I'm asking for."

"And what if I'm not there one day?"

"What if I'm not?" Audrey said. "You learn to move on. That's all you can do."

"You've changed. That young playful girl has been replaced by the woman in front of me."

"I grew up, Charley. You're not the only one in adult pants anymore. I had to grow up very fast. I literally spend most of my days trying to keep people alive that are burnt all over, missing limbs, and hanging on to life by a string. I've seen so much death in the last six months I can't even begin to describe it. You've been directly in the middle of these attacks and I've been handling the aftermath. There's no reason why either of us should go through this hell alone, not when we have each other."

Charley pulled Audrey up into her lap and kissed her lips softly. When Audrey deepened the kiss, sliding her tongue between Charley's lips, Charley laid back with Audrey on top of her.

Breaking the kiss Audrey said, "Can anyone see us?"

Charley shrugged and grinned.

"What if we get caught?"

"I guess we'll buy a little place on the edge of town somewhere near the water and set up house," Charley said nonchalantly.

Audrey laughed and shook her head. "What's happened to you?"

"You. Audrey, you happened to me."

Audrey unbuttoned Charley's uniform jacket. Running her hand under her khaki t-shirt, she squeezed Charley's breast softly.

Charley had never been with a woman that wanted her as much as she wanted them and she loved every minute of it. Reaching her hand between them, she found the edge of Audrey's seersucker uniform skirt and pulled it up. Sliding her hand inside the edge of Audrey's panties, she ran her fingers through the wetness she knew was waiting for her. Audrey gasped, sliding against Charley's fingers pressing against her.

Audrey leaned back slightly looking down at Charley. "Your uniform," she said.

"What about it?" Charley asked, stroking her again.

"It'll get all messy," Audrey melted into the touch.

Charley grinned. "It'll wash," she said, pushing her fingers inside Audrey's tight opening.

Audrey moaned, her body moved on its own against the pressure inside her. Panting, she rode Charley's fingers back and forth, harder, taking her deeper with each thrust.

Charley rose enough to run her lips and tongue over Audrey's neck going as low as she could, meeting the uniform top. Audrey ran her hand over Charley's chest, squeezing her breasts back and forth, matching each movement of her hips.

Charley pulled her fingers out when she felt Audrey getting close. Audrey gasped in protest. Charley pushed Audrey's hips up and moved her forward enough to slide further under her.

"What are we doing?" Audrey whispered.

"Trust me," Charley said, maneuvering Audrey's hips over her shoulders. Reaching up, she pulled Audrey's sex to her mouth, licking each wet fold back and forth.

"Oh my god," Audrey called out loudly.

Charley licked lazy circles around her clit, sucking it in with every pass. Audrey's hips moved against her face urging her further. Charley knew her own body couldn't wait much longer. She was wet and throbbing.

Audrey stilled when she heard the zipper on Charley's pants. She reached back feeling Charley's hand inside her own pants as she began stroking herself. Audrey moved off of Charley's face.

"What are you doing?" Charley whispered.

"Trust me." Audrey grinned. Turning her position around, she moved back over Charley's face and leaned forward pulling her hand free. She pushed Charley's pants and underwear down enough to see the wetness glistening in the moonlight. Bending her head down, she pressed her tongue to Charley's clit and licked, tasting another woman for the first time.

Her tongue tingled and Charley's hips jerked. She licked a little harder, feeling Charley pull her hips down, matching her lick for lick. When Charley sucked her she sucked Charley's clit. They traded licks and sucks, moving back and forth, each woman panting and gasping, but never stopping her assault on the others sex.

Audrey came first, jerking her hips and trembling as the waves of orgasm washed over her body. Charley quickly followed, grunting and pushing her hips hard into Audrey's face, begging for more as her body finally gave way.

The salty cool breeze stung their exposed skin when they parted. Charley pulled Audrey down for a searing kiss, mixing their tastes together on their tongues.

"Where did you learn that?" Charley asked breathlessly when their lips separated.

Audrey shrugged. "I don't know. I've never done that before. You know you're the only one..."

"Still?" Charley asked.

"Always. I only want you and only you, Charley."

Charley smiled and kissed her again slowly, taking the time to enjoy the beautiful woman in her arms. Audrey pulled back to look at her as Charley ran her hand over Audrey's soft cheek.

"I love you," Audrey whispered.

"I love you, too." Charley swallowed the lump in her throat. Sighing, she said, "You should probably get going before you get caught being out after lights out."

"I think we're pulling anchor in the morning. I don't know when I'll see you again," Audrey said, wiping a tear from her cheek.

"Write me."

"You never write back."

"I will this time. I promise." Charley smiled.

Chapter Seventeen

Two weeks had gone by since the USHS *Solace* steamed away from Midway Island taking Charley's heart with it. She should be happy, her squadron received new orders, they were finally going stateside away from the crosshairs of the Japanese, but deep in the back of her mind she was wondering if and when she would ever see Audrey again. She emptied her footlocker, neatly stuffing its contents into her Army-issued green duffle bag. She donned her Dress Uniform, spit-shined her shoes one last time, and put on her garrison cap before walking out of the barracks and away from the war zone for the last time.

Charley's squadron was being transferred to Chico Army Airfield in Northern California. It was actually a huge privilege to be sent there. CAA was the Army Air Force training base for all of its pilots and thus booming with activity. Hundreds of new pilots were training every day to beef up the US fleet and new planes were set to begin delivery from the factories over the next few months. More planes meant more service personnel, which was another reason Charley's squadron was being sent there.

No, she wouldn't be in the 'hot zone' on the frontlines of the Pacific any longer, but Charley knew her workload was about to quadruple taking on a base of that size with close to four-hundred planes. Of course, her squadron wouldn't be the only active service squadron, as it never was anywhere she was stationed, but the amount of planes on her log books was about to go up to numbers she couldn't even dream of. She still hadn't told the squadron of the new changes, only mentioning that they were going stateside to a base in California.

Her orders indicated her squadron would grow to thirty members as soon as she landed with the possibility of getting even larger as the war efforts continued. She would be in charge of the maintenance and service for two new fleets that were arriving just behind her, as well as training a completely new female service squadron.

Charley saw the large transport plane land and taxi towards the fuel depot close to where her hangar was. She threw her duffle over her shoulder and pulled her cap down tight as she began walking towards the plane.

"Major! Wait up!" Patterson shouted, running out of the barracks behind her.

"I figured you would be with the rest of the squadron. Higs was supposed to have everyone ready to board our bird ten minutes ago," Charley chided.

"I know. I'm sorry, ma'am. I was reading a letter from home that I got this morning and I lost track of time." Patterson fell instep next to Charley with her head hung low.

"Want to talk about?" Charley asked, hoping the young corporal would say no. That was one of the bad parts of being an officer or especially the commander of a squadron full of young women. They wore their hearts on their sleeves and often times found themselves very homesick. She'd had to play mom on more than one occasion. Charley noticed a lot of that with her group when they first arrived at Pearl Harbor, but slowly they'd learned to become soldiers.

"Not much to talk about, really. My little sister who graduated high school last summer married her high school sweetheart just before Thanksgiving and found out recently that she is pregnant with their first child. That was supposed to be me. My parents had my life all planned out the same way. I was going to marry Thomas Newman when we graduated high school and he would go to work at his daddy's lumber yard and hopefully take over the business one day. My mom wants a house full of grandchildren and made sure I knew that she'd expected one right away once we were married. I was going to be just like her, a housewife with five children, and leader of the church choir." Patterson kicked a rock as she walked by it.

"How did you wind up in the Army Air Force if that was already planned out for you?"

Patterson sighed, "I didn't want to marry Thomas. I didn't even like him. I was much more interested in his sister Evelyn."

"I see," Charley said. She had a feeling she knew where this was going. She remembered Higs talking about Patterson being a 'sister' but she didn't believe it.

"I graduated from school and joined the service two months after my birthday. My parents were furious and my father tried everything to get me out, but it was too late. I ran away from everything and broke my mom's heart because I couldn't tell them the truth."

"What did they say to you in the letter?"

"Not much, my mom just says over and over how disappointed she is and how she doesn't think women should be in the service and she goes on and on about the war. Thomas married some other girl about a year ago, I guess. My mom says it's because he didn't want to wait for me."

"I'm surprised he's not in the service with the war going on."

"He can't pass the physical. He has a bad knee from playing football and getting injured. He had surgery but it didn't fully correct it. He walks with a limp."

They were getting closer to the waiting plane and Higs had all of the women lined up in formation.

Charley knew what it was like to have a demanding mother that didn't understand your views. She wasn't sure what to tell Patterson because instead of standing up and fighting with her own mother she'd simply joined the military and left without looking back. Every letter sent to her said the same thing over and over. Her mother always told her she needed to come home and be a proper lady and give up this foolishness. After the letter that her mother wrote saying she was shaming her dead father by doing what she was doing Charley quit reading the letters.

Charley stopped walking and Patterson turned around to face her.

"Everything happens for a reason, Patterson. Maybe one day your parents will see their mistakes and be proud of their daughter and her service to their country. I know I'm proud of you every single day. You've improved so much since I first met you as a private first class with absolutely no idea what direction you were going in. You never faltered through two attacks in the middle of this war and you're a survivor. No one would understand what that is like except for the people that were there with you. You're a huge part of this squadron, whether you realize it or not, and it's okay to be a little different. Think about how dull life would be if we were all the same boring Suzie homemaker."

"Thanks, Major." Patterson smiled.

"Go get into formation so we can get this bird off the ground," Charley said. She watched Patterson run ahead and join the group.

"Everyone is present and accounted for, ma'am," said Higs.

"Good. I don't know about all of you, but I sure as hell am ready to be off this island."

The women cheered and Higs raised her hand to quiet them back down.

"When we arrive there will be a short briefing and then we will be shown around. I want everyone to pay attention to their surroundings because this is by far the largest base you will ever see. More than likely we will be confined to one of the five auxiliary fields, which is perfectly fine with me. Also, there will be another dozen or so women joining our squadron so let's welcome them with open arms and show them the way the we operate." Charley stepped back and waited for the group to salute her. She returned their salute and dismissed them to board the plane.

"Why are we doubling in size?" Higs asked.

"We're going to Chico and we're the main service squadron for two different fleets stationed at the auxiliary fields. I'm almost sure that's where we will be too. We needed the extra personnel. Oh and to top it off, we're getting another squadron of twenty something females to train as a service squadron."

"Wow. As if we haven't had enough shit on our plates lately. Chico?" Higs shook her head.

"No kidding. Listen, Higs, I will be making some rank adjustments during the first week so I need your input on who you think is promotable, yourself included."

"Yes, ma'am." Higs saluted and boarded the plane.

***

After two short stops for fuel, they completed the long flight and touched down just after dark. Charley thanked the pilots and climbed out of the plane last. Her squadron once again stood in formation waiting to be addressed.

"Good evening, Major. Welcome to Chico Army Airfield. We're glad to have your squadron here with us." An older gentleman wearing an Army officer's uniform similar to Charley's shook her hand. He was one of the base colonels and her commanding officer.

"Thank you, Colonel. It's nice to be stateside again."

"I've arranged for you ladies to be taken to the mess hall for some chow, and then shown to your barracks building for the night. As you know, Chico has a main airfield which is this one here, and we have one auxiliary field, Kirkwood Auxiliary Airfield. We are in the process of building four more auxiliary fields that will be used as crash sites, bombing training sites, and so on. There will only be service at Kirkwood, so your squadron will be stationed there. We have a mess hall, officers' buildings, commissary, hospital, dispensary, multiple barracks, a chapel, five hangars, and a number of classroom buildings here at the main field. You will find a small mess hall, barracks building, classroom buildings, fuel depot, oil tank, and a double hangar out at Kirkwood. That airfield is about eighteen miles away so you may also get ferried planes from time to time."

"Each member of your squadron will receive updated vaccines since you've been overseas and in combat. Also, all squadron CO's receive a service Jeep, so you will get that in the morning as well. There are yard trucks in the motor pool and other various means of transportation for all of the enlisted members stationed throughout the base. You will receive those schedules too. So, if there are no questions, let's go get you ladies some chow and a rack for the night."

"Talk about a change of scenery. I'm not sure because it's dark, but I think those are mountains," Higs said when the colonel walked away.

"Yes, Higs, those are mountains. Okay, you heard the colonel. Let's double-time into the yard truck. I'm starving," Charley said.

Chapter Eighteen

Charley walked out of the barracks and breathed in the fresh mountain air. She didn't miss the salt from the islands one bit. She stretched her back and eased down the steps towards her Jeep. Her squadron was the only service squadron stationed at Kirkwood Auxiliary Airfield, but there were two fighter training squadrons also stationed there with them. Charley had wondered why the two groups would be singled out away from the rest of the training squadrons stationed at Chico, but her answer came quickly when she'd arrived at the double hangar.

"You are not going to believe this," Higs ran over to the Jeep before Charley could get it stopped.

"What's wrong?"

"Keep driving," Higs said, jumping into the passenger seat.

Charley downshifted and rounded the corner. "What's got your panties all in a wad?"

"Have you seen the flight trainers?"

"Oh, yeah the Valiant's." Charley laughed, rolling her eyes. The trainer planes were B-13 and B-15

Valiant's, painted bright blue with yellow wings and tails. They looked like circus planes and were extremely slow and boring to fly.

"No, not the damn blue planes...the black pilots!"

Charley slammed the breaks causing Higs to lurch forward into the dash.

"Excuse me?"

"You heard me. Colored pilots!"

"No shit?"

"No shit!"

"Well, something definitely happened in the States while we were gone. That's for sure," Charley said, putting the Jeep back in gear and proceeding down the road. She'd barely seen any colored men the entire time she'd been in the service, and those she did see had been mostly cooks.

"I'm surprised they don't have a colored service squadron," Higs said.

"Yeah, that is a little odd. Maybe they don't know how to fix planes."

"Well, they're sure as hell learning to fly them." Higs laughed.

"I wouldn't laugh just yet. We're doubling as the fire fighters on this field and the last thing we need is a bunch of planes crashing around us. We'll have our hands full enough as it is keeping these planes in the air and training that new squadron. By the way, they should be arriving next week sometime so be prepared for that. As far as I know they've been through mechanic school and that's it."

"Wonderful, black pilots and green mechanics." Higs shook her head. "And don't get me started on the Valiant trainers. We just spent the last year working on fighter

132

planes in the 'hot zone' and now we get to come home and work on these pieces of shit," she said, jumping out of the Jeep when they stopped near the hangar.

***

Charley was looking over the log sheets for the fifty planes in her fleet when there was knock on her office door. She pulled it open and stepped back when she saw a colored man in an Army officer's uniform standing in her doorway.

"Good afternoon. I'm Maj. Henry Jones. I'm the CO for the 354th Flight Group. Your squadron will be servicing both of my flight groups training squadrons here at Kirkwood."

"Yes, that is correct. I'm Maj. Charlotte Hayes." Charley stuck her hand out.

It was the first time she'd ever touched the skin of a colored person before and she wondered if it was even appropriate. Either way, he grabbed her hand with his and shook back. His skin was rough and thick like a tough piece of meat.

"I look forward to working with you. Each squadron has a captain as their squadron leader. They should be around sometime today to introduce themselves."

"Can I ask you something? Why isn't there a colored service squadron working with your group?"

"There aren't any, I guess. We are one of the first colored flight groups allowed by the Army Air Force. The other groups were sent to Alabama."

"I see."

"Are we going to have a problem here, Major?" he asked.

"No, not at all. My squadron just got back from serving overseas for a year so we were a little shocked to see a colored flight group, that's all."

"Yes, I heard you were at Pearl and Midway when they were bombed."

Charley nodded.

"I hope one day we get to see combat. This isn't the white man's war. This is America's war and everyone wants to be a part of it, men, women, white, black, everyone."

"I can't argue with that. I'm just glad to be out of the middle of it to be honest with you. A person can only handle planes shooting at you and dropping bombs on your head a limited number of times." She grinned.

"I wouldn't know. I've been working a desk since I joined. But, with the success of this new flight group I hope all of that is about to change."

"Good luck to you and your group. I think we will work well together," Charley said.

When Maj. Jones left the hangar Higs stormed into Charley's office.

"Was that a colored officer?"

"Yes it was. That's Maj. Jones, the CO of the colored flight group."

"I never thought I'd see the day," she said, shaking her head.

"Higs, we're not going to have a problem working with the coloreds, are we?"

"No," she said, shaking her head. "It's just a little shocking, that's all. I'm from the deep south and coloreds do nothing but cook, clean, and tend to the grounds. They damn sure don't fly planes or wear officer's uniforms."

"It's about the same where I'm from too, but America is changing and we have to roll with the changes. I need you to ask around and make sure everyone is clear that we will not have any issues with the coloreds. That's an order."

"Yes, ma'am." Higs saluted.

"It looks like our new squadron members are arriving," Charley pointed out the window of the office where a group of women were walking into the hangar. "Get them all settled in as quickly as you can. We will evaluate their skills and pair them up with the other girls."

"That's what I was planning on doing."

"What do you think of Patterson?"

"What do you mean?" asked Higs.

"Do you think she's ready to move up and lead the squadron?"

"What about me?" Higs raised her eyebrows.

"With those trainees coming in next week I will need a Technical Sergeant leading them. If I move you up in rank then I need someone to take your place. I also need to make a few more adjustments too. I think we have some privates that need to be made corporals and some that need to be moved up to technician fifth grade."

"I'm not sure about Patterson. Let me work with her a little bit this week and give her some extra leadership duties on top of what she's already doing and see how it goes. She's doing very well as a sergeant though."

"We need to look at moving someone to technician third grade to assist you. You decide who you want and get back to me by Friday with all of these changes. I will turn in your review and adjust your rank this weekend."

135

"Yes, ma'am." Higs saluted and left the office when she was dismissed. Being promoted again was exciting and become a technical sergeant was what she'd been striving so hard to achieve. To become a technical sergeant meant you had to know the technicalities of your job inside and out and be able to lead others in a technical format. Being a staff sergeant was basically a job managing the squadron personnel and she knew Patterson would be good at that position if she learned to trust herself more.

***

Charley finished assigning the planes on her log sheet just before the end of the day. She was glad to have a larger squadron, but that meant twice as many planes she was directly responsible for. She could only imagine how many indirectly. At Pearl Harbor and Midway, her squadron had had fifteen to twenty planes that they were the actual service squadron for, the rest of the planes they'd repaired were from other air groups and other branches of the military that used them as easy labor so her group knew what it was like servicing a large number of planes at certain times. She hoped they could handle doing it on a daily basis, and with a training group working right next to them.

Chapter Nineteen

Close to a month had gone by since Charley's squadron had arrived at Chico and was sub-stationed at Kirkwood. Everyone was settling into their new ranks and new positions within her squadron and the trainees were beginning to work on planes. They'd spent their first two weeks learning how to be fire fighters. The women were the only firefighting personnel at the airfield. Charley wanted them to know the basics and learn the same way she had and the same way she'd taught her own girls.

"Open up!" Higs was pounding on the door to Charley's room over and over. Charley watched patiently from her position down the hall.

"It's not going to open itself," she finally said.

Higs jumped a foot off the ground, grabbing her chest as she squealed. "You scared the shit out of me."

"Well, you're beating on my door like a rabid baboon. What is so damn important?"

"This!" Higs held the letter up in Charley's face so closely she could barely read her name on the front. She snatched it and put it in her room on the tiny desk.

"You're not going to read it? It's from Audrey."

"I know who it's from. I'm going to the mess hall to get my dinner before it closes. I just stopped in to get another pack of smokes when I found you terrorizing my door."

"I thought you were going to quit."

"I am. I've done it before, it doesn't exactly happen overnight," Charley growled.

"Well, give me one then. I traded mine to the colored pilots for a little bottle of hooch they've mixed up."

Charley shook her head and laughed. "You don't smoke and hooch is nasty. Stay away from that stuff."

"I need more trading material and as if you haven't noticed the States are going through some kind of rationing craze so there's a shortage of real alcohol, at least there is on the damn base. I miss being overseas."

"I miss a lot of things. Like, oh I don't know, peace and quiet," Charley huffed.

"Fine, go enjoy your dinner. They served fried chicken, mashed potatoes, and some kind of greens tonight. Anyway, it was much better than that slop we used to get on Midway when the supply ship was late, that's for sure."

Charley had to agree that the food at Kirkwood was definitely much better. She wondered if it was because the mess hall on the small airfield was manned by mostly colored men. She guessed it was probably because they weren't going to have white folks cooking for the coloreds.

***

The sun had barely risen when Charley finished buttoning the jacket of her work uniform. She reached under her pillow and pulled out the letter from Audrey that she'd read twice already the night before and read it again.

Dear Charley,

We heard recently that the German Luftwaffe bombed a British hospital ship. Everyone's nervous and scared. No one is really telling us anything, only that we are safe and not to worry. Fran is about to pull her hair out worrying, so them telling us not to worry really isn't helping much. I was glad to hear you were re-stationed stateside. Maybe the Japs will stay away from you finally. I know you must be happy.

If I have any say in my next assignment, I'm going to ask to go back stateside as well. I know they are making changes daily and every time we stop in San Francisco we lose a few nurses and gain others. I think the ones we are losing are going to the frontlines. The number of wounded soldiers is doubling daily. Last week, we were so packed we actually had patients in our crew quarters hooked up to IV lines with morphine drips because they were missing limbs and had serious infections from the lack of medical care in the field. Which is why they are sending up more nurses.

The ship is a mess. It's a war zone all of its own. I've never mopped so much blood in my life. Between the Pearl Harbor attack and now working on this ship it seems like red is becoming a permanent color on our uniforms. Oh Charley, how I miss you. I hate to write you with the torrid details of my daily life when I know yours can't be much better. Fran tells me Higs said you all are working with colored pilots! My grandmother would just roll out of her southern church pew and die if I wrote home and told her I was working with colored doctors. I can only imagine what it's like for all of you. I wasn't raised too far south, but my father was and his mother is an ornery old cuss.

My next shift is beginning soon and I must say goodbye. I believe we are heading to Guam from wherever we are at the moment. I haven't seen the sun in four days and I'm uncertain as to where we dropped anchor. I will try to get another letter to you when we make port again. I miss you and love you.

Yours Always,
Audrey

Charley folded the letter neatly and slipped it back into the envelope. She left the barracks early to meet a couple of trainers being flown over from another base along with spare parts she had been waiting on. Since Chico had become the pilot training center they were always in need of planes and parts to fix the planes the rookie pilots crashed or misused.

"Hot date?" Higs yawned in the hallway.

"Yes, as a matter of fact I do have a date, with a very sexy pair of Valiant's who are also carrying my much needed parts to rebuild a landing gear and a tail rudder on two planes our wonderful colored pilots destroyed last week."

"Here I thought it was something exciting," Higs rolled her eyes.

"Are your girls ready to go solo yet?"

"It's only been three weeks."

"They were trained at mechanics school for at least eight weeks. They should know what the tools are, how to change the oil in anything, how to check and adjust fluid levels, how to refuel anything, and how to repair a hydraulic system. Our job is to teach them how to do it as a group and how to do it efficiently especially in the midst of chaos."

"Remember back to when you first started with me, I tested everything you learned at mechanics school, then took it two or three levels higher teaching you how to do it twice as fast with more proficiency. That is what you should be doing with those girls. Don't babysit them. We aren't here to babysit and if they can't cut it, they're out."

Charley moved out of the doorway, but turned back around. "If I wasn't stern with you girls and taught you the way I did, we would have never made it through two battles. Cpl. Lowe paid the ultimate price, but it wasn't because of her training. If anything, she was doing her duty trying to get that plane going so another pilot could fight for us. Never forget what it was like and hopefully these women will be prepared for something they will never see."

***

Charley thought she'd been surprised when she saw colored pilots, but she was shocked when the two blue and yellow trainers rolled to a stop near her hangar with what looked like women climbing out of the cockpits. She blinked her eyes and looked again. There was no mistaking the subtle curve of a woman's breasts and hips. Those two pilots were women.

141

"You must be Maj. Hayes." one of the women said as she removed her flight cap, shaking out her light brown hair.

"That's correct." Charley cleared her throat, still a little stunned. "When did the Army start allowing women to fly?" she asked.

The other woman laughed. "We're civilians. They call us Women Airforce Service Pilots. We ferry planes and parts all over from base to base and from the factories to the bases. I'm Gladys Monroe, by the way and this is Mary White."

"I see. It's nice to meet you," Charley said, helping them remove the extra parts from the planes. "I haven't been stateside long, I just got back from a little over a year overseas, so forgive me for not knowing about your service."

"Where were you stationed?" Gladys asked..

"Pearl Harbor and Midway," Charley replied.

"Were you there during the attacks?" Mary's eyebrows were nearly in her dark hairline.

Charley nodded.

"Wow. I'd heard there were women there, but I figured nurses and such," Mary said.

"What was it like?" Gladys asked.

Charley sighed. She hated talking about it. "It was about how they said it was on the radios and in the papers, I guess, very chaotic, with lots of bombs, strafing rounds, and explosions. The air was so thick with rancid, heavy black smoke you could barely see anything. Midway wasn't anywhere near as bad as Pearl as far as damage and death, but it was still bad enough."

"Here comes our ride," Mary said, pointing to the yard truck the motor pool had sent for them.

"I'm glad we got to meet you, Major. I hope we see each other again," Gladys said, shaking Charley's hand. When the truck drove away, another truck pulled up behind it, dropping off her squadron.

"I see you got your planes and parts," Higs said.

"Yes I did and you will never believe me when I say they were flown by two women pilots."

"No, they were not."

"Oh yes they were. I think it's called Women Airforce Service Pilots or something like that. They're civilians though," Charley said.

"I will believe that when I see it. I think you're trying to bet me out of my smokes or something." Higs grinned.

"Why would I do that? I said I was quitting. I've barely had any this week. I think my stress level has lowered tremendously since we've been here. I'm not looking over my shoulder anymore for Japs."

"I still don't believe you. Then again, we have colored pilots here so they must be giving pilots licenses to anyone these days." Higs shrugged and looked at the blue sky. "Don't mention the damn Japs. If they find us here I'm moving to Canada!" she growled, walking away.

***

Charley was watching a blue and yellow Valiant trainer flying overhead and enjoying a leisurely walk back to the hangar after having a late lunch at the mess hall. Her mind was focusing on the two planes she needed to finish repairing before the end of the day while her thoughts were on the letter sitting under the pillow in her room that she was writing to Audrey. Suddenly, the plane dipped too low and the rookie pilot overcorrected pulling back too hard on the stick and the plane stalled at around five-hundred feet. She could hear the engine sputter as the pilot frantically tried to restart it as the plane swirled closer to the ground.

"Get out!" she shouted waving her hands and arms back and forth trying to get the solo pilot to bail out of the plane.

The engine finally caught and turned over just as the plane smashed into the ground, exploding into a giant ball of fire. Charley was already running towards the fire truck parked close to her hangar. Higs had seen the plane going down and already had part of the squadron putting on their turnout gear when it crashed.

"Let's go," she shouted.

They met Charley at the truck and drove as quickly as they could towards the burning wreckage in the middle of the airfield. The fire was extremely hot with thick orange flames and heavy black smoke. The women pulled the hoses out and began hooking up the lines just as they'd practiced.

"He didn't even try to bail out," Higs said, watching the squadron douse the flames.

"I'm surprised he was flying solo. Where the hell was his instructor?" Charley looked around and finally saw the Jeep heading in her direction.

"What a disaster," Maj. Jones said, climbing from the Jeep.

"Where was his instructor?"

"Up in the tower. They started solo takeoff and landing routines this week," he said.

"He must have been trying to land when he overcorrected and stalled it," Charley said.

"Yes. His instructor advised him to try one restart and bail if it didn't catch," he said, shaking his head. "Damn kid kept saying he could get it started. He never even looked at the altimeter."

The fire was just about out when some of the other training pilots arrived at the crash site. Charley and Higs dressed in their turnout gear and went to retrieve the body when the last of the smoldering wreckage was extinguished. A couple of the pilots ran over to help, but Charley shook her head no. She didn't want them to see the body burnt beyond recognition and the temperature was still extremely hot. She and Higs pulled the body out and placed it in a black bag. Charley reached inside and removed the pilots metal wings from his flight suit before zipping the bag closed. They walked past the group of pilots who stood at attention, saluting their fallen brother along with everyone from Charley's service squadron and loaded the bag on the back of Maj. Jones' Jeep. He was taking care of the arrangements.

"What was his name?" Charley asked when she walked back over to Maj. Jones.

"Cadet William 'Willie' Buford," he said.

Charley unzipped her turnout coat; pulling a rag from her pocket she wrapped it around the warm wings.

"Cadet Buford's parents will probably want these," she said, handing them to Maj. Jones.

Chapter Twenty

A month went by without any more severe accidents. Charley was about to sign off on the training squadron and release them to regular duty just in time to receive a new training squadron right behind them. She wondered if this was how it was going to be for the rest of her time in the Army Air Force, or the rest of the war, whichever came first. She didn't exactly mind either way. It was busy work and it was for a good cause. She didn't miss being in the 'hot zone', but she did miss working on the planes from the front lines. They often presented a challenge and that kept her on her toes and made her job exciting. Valiant trainers were about as boring as military airplanes could get and she could take one apart and put it back together with her eyes closed.

Charley finished the paperwork she'd been signing and called Higs into her office. The sun was starting to rise over the mountains behind the base, painting the sky in hues of orange and yellow.

"You weren't kidding when you said be here before sun up. What's so exciting I had to drag my butt out of bed an hour early?"

"Nothing really," Charley shrugged. "I usually come in this early to get caught up on paperwork and other official office duties. I wanted to let you know I am releasing your training squadron to regular duty, so you can give them the good news this morning and go ahead and get them transferred out today. The new training squadron is coming in a week early since this group has been released."

"Wow, I was expecting the end of the week. I'll get them transferred out this afternoon. They're being attached to a flight group on the East Coast and who knows from there."

"That's good. I know they are sending a few flight groups to Italy soon," Charley said.

"Are we going?" Higs asked.

"No. This is our home for the next year maybe two. Hell, we may even be here until the war ends. I have no idea. I just know we're not on the transfer docket for another year for sure."

"That's good," Higs sighed.

"I miss it too," Charley said.

The rest of the women began arriving and the hangar came alive with the hustle and bustle of the morning.

"Hey Major, there's a half a dozen planes coming this way," Patterson said when Higs opened the office door.

"They're not Japanese planes are they?" Higs said, walking vigorously past her towards the open bay doors.

"No. Not unless they painted their planes blue and yellow," Patterson yelled back.

"It's the new B-15 version of the trainers coming in from the factory," Charley explained as she joined Higs and Patterson outside.

The brightly painted planes landed single file and taxied towards the rest of the training fleet sitting on the ready line. One by one each pilot climbed out, took her flight cap off, and shook her hair out.

"They're women!" Higs exclaimed.

Charley laughed. "I tried to tell you about them."

The women walked the short distance to the service hangar where all of Charley's squadron was standing outside watching them.

"Major," Gladys saluted and handed Charley the updated schematics that the factory forgot to put in the new manual.

Charley took the papers and saluted back. "Gladys and Mary, this is Army Air Force Service Squadron-Thirteen and my command."

The women exchanged names and handshakes as Gladys introduced the other pilots that were flying with her and Mary. Higs and Patterson asked a hundred questions while the pilots waited for their yard truck.

"So you ferry planes and parts back and forth to the factories?" Patterson asked.

"Yes. We take new planes to training bases or to other bases close to the front lines and bring back planes that need more work than can be done in the field at most of the forward fighting bases. We also deliver parts all over," Gladys said.

"And you're civilians?" Higs asked.

"Yes. Hopefully, one day they see us more than women like they do all of you and allow us to wear their wings," Mary said.

"I would love to see combat," one of the other pilots said.

"It's overrated and sounds more exciting than the hell that it really is," Patterson said.

Charley patted her shoulder and moved to answer the ringing phone in her office. She was so proud of Patterson. She'd seen her grow from a young naive girl into a strong woman over the past year and a half. War seemed to age everyone at a high rate of speed.

Charley took the quick call and walked back out to the group of women.

"It looks like you ladies are hanging out with us today. They have a group of training bombers over at Chico that need to be moved to the new auxiliary base. It's a bombing training base with only a tower. There's no one actually stationed there. They just finished laying the runway a few days ago, I think. Anyway, since our training squadron is on their way out of here this afternoon, you ladies are going to stay over in their barracks tonight after you finish moving their planes around at Chico and a transport plane will be here in the morning to get you."

"It's a party," Higs said with a grin. "I hope you ladies play poker."

Charley shook her head and laughed.

***

Charley sat at the tiny desk in her room preparing to write a letter to Audrey. She'd played poker until she won close to a week's pay and had decided not to take anymore of everyone's money. She'd taken a quick shower and retired to her room for the night. The pilots settled in nicely at the barracks next door, but they all came over to play poker.

Dear Audrey,

I hope this letter finds you in better spirits than the last one. Life has sure turned around for me and my squadron. We've settled in nicely, almost too nicely. I don't miss being in the middle of the war, not at all. Higs and I do however, both miss the excitement of being close and working with real planes. Working on trainers has just about bored me out of my mind.

We did have some excitement today actually. A group of new planes arrived from the factory and they were piloted by a civilian women's ferry service. They got stuck here overnight so as I write to you at this moment Higs and a few of my other girls are desperately trying to take their money playing poker. I bowed out after winning eight out of ten hands. Maybe I will buy myself a nice bottle of whiskey with my winnings since I quit smoking. You'll be glad to hear that I'm sure.

Last month, one of the colored pilots crashed during a training exercise and burned to death. I think that really put everyone into perspective, especially the service squadron training with us. Most of those girls took it pretty hard, but the girls in my squadron talked with them about losing one of their own and what it was like to pick up the pieces and keep going because the war doesn't stop when someone dies unfortunately. No one knows about that more than you and the girls you work with. It takes a strong person to do what you do every day.

Working with the coloreds actually has some advantages. The only white folk on our base are us and the instructors. They aren't as egotistic as the white pilots and they sure can cook some food. I think I've actually gained a couple of pounds!

I should go break up that poker game or I will be working alone tomorrow. Those girls would stay up all night playing cards if I let them. I look forward to reading your next letter. I miss you and love you always.

With Love,
Charley

Charley folded the letter neatly, slipped it into the envelope, and set it on the corner of the desk so she would remember to post it in the morning on the way to the hangar. She pulled a pair of pants and a shirt on over her underclothes and walked down the hallway towards the noise.

Chapter Twenty-One

Charley walked into the hangar with a smile on her face and a little pep in her step after posting her latest letter to Audrey. It wasn't easy worrying about her floating around the 'hot zone' in the middle of the war, but knowing she was out there and that she loved Charley as much as she loved her somehow made it tolerable.

"You seem happy this morning. Did they slip something into your breakfast at the mess hall?" Higs asked.

Charley rolled her eyes. "Not that it's any of your business, but I posted a letter this morning and I may not be in this great mood for long so don't tempt me. I take it our flying friends got off okay this morning?"

"Yes. The yard truck picked them up on time to meet their plane over at Chico. You missed a hell of a poker game. You won't believe it, but three of them are 'sisters'."

Charley stopped looking at the repair list for the plane she was scheduled to work on and spun around on her heels.

"Tell me you didn't mention my name."

"No. I didn't have to. Gladys said she knew right away," Higs said.

"Oh wonderful. Let me guess, you told them all about Audrey and Fran too. Am I right?"

"Nope. I told them about Fran, but I didn't say anything about Audrey. I know how skittish you are. I just wish you would realize we aren't alone. There are other people like us out there in the world and in this war."

"I know there are, Higs, but there are still a lot of people including some in this hangar right now that don't understand our way of life and would soon enough see us run up the flag pole by our hair. Just be careful who you tell or talk to about it and always make sure you know who is within listening distance because you never know who will turn on you."

"I know what you mean. I steer clear of the assholes. It's hard not to be excited to meet other people like us though. I'm from a small town and I only knew one other 'sister' and even then I'm not even sure if she was or not. She was an old hermit that lived alone on the edge of the river. I've met at least a half a dozen 'sisters' since I've been in the service."

Charley nodded. "Just be careful," she said. She couldn't argue with Higs, it was nice to know you weren't alone in the world with your differences.

Higs went back to the plane she had been working on and Charley was about to climb up into the cockpit of the Valiant trainer she was standing next to when Patterson came running into the hangar. She was completely out of breath and frantically waving a piece of paper.

"What's wrong?" Higs said, grabbing the paper. She quickly read the short paragraph and dropped to her knees.

"What is it?" Charley snatched the paper.

Army Air Force Confidential Document 0812539:

At 0300 Pacific Time the USHS *Solace* was dive bombed by a Japanese plane causing a massive explosion mid-ship on the portside. The ship began taking on water and listing heavily to port and finally sunk at approximately 0835 Pacific Time. The USS *Saratoga* from the Pacific Carrier Group received the distress call and responded. There are over fifty casualties, over a hundred injuries, and thirty-five missing or unaccounted for at this time.

Charley balled the paper and tossed it on the floor at her feet as she bent to help Higs up off the floor. "We don't know anything yet, they're probably fine," she said.

Higs wiped the tears from her face. "You're right, we don't know."

Charley knew deep down the day would come for one of them. Love and war didn't mix. She hoped Audrey and Fran were okay and had made it off the ship safely.

"I'll go over to Chico in a little while and see what I can find out. Until then, we have to think positive," Charley said. "We may not know anything for days. How did you even get this report?" she asked Patterson.

"It came into the instructors' office. I was on my way here when Maj. Jones stopped me and asked me to bring this to you. After I read it I knew I couldn't wait for the yard truck so I ran all the way here."

Charley nodded. "We have work to do, ladies. This is just another cruel sign that we are in the middle of a war. Higs, go take a walk and clear your head. Patterson, bring the squadron up to speed on this latest development," she said.

Charley walked into her office and wiped the lone tear that had been threatening to roll down her cheek.

***

Charley could barely concentrate on the plane she was working on. Repairing a canopy latch should only take an hour at most and she'd been at it for two and half hours. Nothing seemed to keep her mind from wandering back to Audrey and the last time she saw her smiling face. She wondered where she was and hoped she was okay. The Army Air Force did their best, training her for her job and teaching her how to be an officer and command a squadron, but no one ever taught her how to deal with the repercussions of war. That's one subject they tended to overlook as if all of the death and destruction is an everyday occurrence and isn't worthy of preparation. Then again, how do you prepare for something that catastrophic?

Charley did her best preparing her squadron for the solemn fact that they could be at war at one point during their service. She even went as far as drilling them on air raid safety, a training lesson that saved their lives on more than one occasion. When they'd lost one of their own she had to teach them how to handle it as soldiers, not friends, and not women. They'd had to stand up and go on like the soldiers they were because the country was at war. There was no time to grieve, no time to think about what had just happened or was happening right over their heads.

Charley was good at pulling her squadron together and leading them through the chaos day in and day out. That was easy because it was her job, it wasn't personal. The one thing Charley wasn't good at was handling the stress of the war on a personal level. Up until now, the only person she'd had to worry about or care about was herself and getting herself through this war. Now, she had Audrey to care about and worry about and knowing something happened to her, but not knowing if she was okay was eating her alive every minute that ticked by. This was the one reason she'd tried so desperately to let go of Audrey. Charley was a good leader, but Audrey had exposed her one weakness...love. She wasn't strong enough to love someone and not know if she would come home to them at the end of her service with a smile on her face or in a wooden box. Audrey being in the service too only made matters worse. Charley didn't want the call or the letter. She didn't want to know if Audrey's life was over.

The wrench Charley was using to tighten the canopy bolts slipped causing her to cut her knuckle.

"Damn it!" she snapped, jumping out of the cockpit. She wrapped her hand with a rag and walked outside of the hangar. The overcast sky was beginning to darken with rain clouds. Charley ran a hand through her hair and put her garrison cap back on as she sat on the bumper of her Jeep. She heard footsteps and turned to see Higs walking towards her.

"I'm okay," she said.

"How's your hand?" Higs said, sitting next to her.

"Fine. It's just a scratch."

"She's alright. They both are. They have to be."

156

Charley sighed. She felt deflated and lost for the first time in her life. She needed to pull it together before the entire squadron noticed.

"You're right. I don't know why I'm letting it bother me so much."

"Because you love her," Higs said.

Charley looked at her and laughed. "You're like a stray cat that won't go away and I'm too stupid to quit feeding it. Meaning I'm too stupid to quit feeding you information."

"Yeah, but you're glad this stray cat has your back and always will."

Charley patted Higs on the shoulder and stood up. "You're right. Come on, we have work to do."

***

A week later, Charley tried to inquire about the sunken hospital ship, but there wasn't much information coming across the wire. It was a Navy ship to begin with and only had thirty Army personnel aboard. There was still no word on whether or not any of them were accounted for. Charley did find out that the survivors were taken to Pearl Harbor and spread out among the nearby hospitals, but she knew it would be useless to try and contact the hospitals. She would just have to sit and wait like everyone else.

Chapter Twenty-Two

Three weeks later, Charley received a letter addressed to her from Pearl Harbor. She held her breath and tore the envelope open. She recognized Audrey's loopy feminine handwriting right away and breathed a sigh of relief.

Dear Charley,

I'm not sure if you've been privy to the news or how much you even know at this point, but our ship was bombed by the Japs and sunk a week ago. A lot of nurses and doctors were injured and about sixty people died. Most of them were patients and a few nurses that happened to be in that area of the ship. It was like a nightmare. It happened in the middle of the night. Fran and I had just finished our late rounds and were heading to our racks when a huge explosion rocked the ship. It began taking on water and was listing so badly we thought for sure she was going over. Thankfully, there was a carrier nearby that helped us. I spent a week on that carrier tending to our patients with next to nothing for supplies. It was a living hell that I never want to go through again.

We arrived back at Pearl yesterday and the patients have been transferred all over the islands because we were full to capacity so they needed beds for about a thousand injured soldiers. I have a lot of cuts and bruises and Fran broke her arm. She's such a good person. She wrapped her arm in a sling and went right to work helping our patients. It wasn't until we arrived on the island that she even realized it was broken. Thankfully, she won't need surgery or anything. They put her in a short cast for a few weeks. She refused to stop working. I don't know how she's doing it. I just want out.

I asked for a transfer stateside. I can't take it anymore. I'm tired of all of this death around me and having my life put on the line. I joined to get nursing experience, not go fight in a war. I kept thinking about you and wondering if you even knew what happened and if you did what you must be thinking not knowing if I was alive or dead. I'm so glad you're stateside and planning to stay there. It was so hard for me when I heard about Midway knowing you were there. I love you so much.

I need to start my shift and make my rounds. We shouldn't be here much longer. I'll write again when I find out where I'm going. I'm thinking a little house out in the country away from planes and ships and islands and this damn war is starting to sound really good to me.

Yours Always,
Audrey

Charley reread the letter and wiped the tears from her face. She couldn't imagine the ordeal that Audrey had been through, but going through two battles herself she knew it wasn't easy. Audrey had every right to want to get away from all of that. Charley tucked the letter back in the envelope and stepped out of her room.

"I told you they were okay." Higs met her in the hallway with a huge smile on her face. "Fran has a broken arm, but she's alive."

"Yeah, Audrey's letter said she broke her arm. It sounds like they went through hell."

"Uh huh and now they're at Pearl. Talk about going full circle. I can't believe it's almost been a year. Something needs to be done about those damn Japs."

"When I was in the Chico command office recently, I heard a few off the record conversations and it sounds like something serious is being planned."

"Well, that's good. I hope we bomb the hell out of them," Higs growled.

"Me too," Charley said.

"Where do you think they will go from here? Hopefully not another damn ship."

"I have no idea. I know Audrey is ready to come back stateside."

"Fran mentioned that too. Do you think they will get stationed here?"

Charley laughed. "I doubt it. Chico is a pilot training base. There isn't much action here for nurses."

Higs shrugged. "I guess you're right. They will probably be sent overseas again. That's where all of the nurses are needed."

"Hey, I'm glad to hear the good news, Major," Patterson said.

"Thanks. Where are you off to in such a hurry?" Charley asked.

Patterson bit the corner of her mouth and grinned. "The ferry pilots are coming in with some parts and I'm going to meet them."

Charley looked at Higs and raised an eyebrow and Higs smiled.

"You were scheduled to be at a meeting this morning at Chico so I told Patterson to take care of the parts delivery for me. The new training squadron is coming in today and I need to go over the log sheets and start assigning planes."

"I see," Charley said.

"Besides," Higs said. "Patterson has a huge crush on Mary."

Charley shook her head and laughed when she saw the color drain from Patterson's face.

"Be careful, Patterson," Charley said. "You never know who is listening in and watching you."

"Yes, ma'am."

"Puppy love," Higs said, watching Patterson run down the hall.

"I seem to recall you acting the same damn way not too long ago, twisting my arm to get you information about Fran and putting in a good word for you."

"Yes, and look where I am today." Higs grinned.

Charley checked her watch. "I'd say late in about two minutes."

"Smartass," Higs said.

Charley walked away and found herself whistling a tune as she drove over to her monthly staff meeting at Chico. She couldn't wipe the smile off her face or stop the pitter patter of her heart. She was learning that love was a mysterious thing with severe highs and lows.

Charley's good mood fizzled out when she walked into the building where her meeting was being held and ran headlong into the two CO's for the service squadrons stationed at Chico.

"Well, if it isn't our little pansy," one of the guys said laughing.

"What's it like working for the coloreds?" the other guy said. "They knew better than to put them here with us. I hear they can't fly worth a shit anyway."

"It probably doesn't help that they have women working on their planes. Maybe that's the problem." the first guy said.

"You can both kiss my ass. If either of you had half the skills my squadron has or flew half as good as those colored pilots you wouldn't be standing here belittling yourselves like school boys. Those colored men have more class and military standards than you'll ever have. Now, if you two will get your scrawny asses out of my way I have work to do," Charley growled.

***

A few days had passed since Charley received the letter from Audrey. She was hard at work repairing the wing on one of the trainers after the pilot had made a miscalculating ground error that morning and smashed his planes wing into a parked plane causing severe damage to both of them. Since these were two of the newer B-15s, Charley and Higs were working together, trying to get them back in the air before the end of the day.

"Clamp that panel and I'll start the rivet line," Charley said, sliding under the corner of the wing near the fuselage with the rivet gun in her hand.

Higs clamped the two sections together and turned to grab more rivets when she heard a loud crash. She spun back around to see Charley in a heap under the heavy wing. She rushed over to help her as two other squadron members began lifting the wing panel.

Charley was barely awake when Higs pulled her limp body away from the plane. Her face was soaked with blood from a cut Higs couldn't locate.

"I'm okay," Charley whispered.

"No, you're not," Higs argued, wiping the blood from her face. "You're bleeding pretty badly and I can't find the cut."

"My head hurts like hell," Charley said, trying to sit up.

"Don't move. You whacked yourself pretty good. Just hold still for a minute."

"I didn't do shit. The half-assed clamp job of yours obviously failed," Charley growled.

"Go get SSgt. Patterson," Higs said to one of the other girls. She kept flipping the rag over and sopping up the blood as it ran down Charley's forehead.

"Oh no," Patterson said, running up to them. "Major, are you okay?"

"I'm fine, Patterson. How are you?" Charley winced when she tried to roll her eyes.

"I need to take her to the hospital," Higs said.

"Maybe we should call the medics," Patterson said.

"Oh no you don't. I'm okay," Charley said trying once again to get up.

"You need to be still," Higs growled.

164

"I agree with her, Major. You have a nasty cut somewhere on your head."

"Here it is," Higs said, pushing Charley's hair off her forehead revealing a large gash.

"Eww, that looks bad," Patterson grimaced at the open cut with dark blood caked around it.

"You definitely need stitches and I'm sure you have a concussion," Higs stated.

Charley sighed and closed her eyes. Her head was pounding in her ears to the rhythm of her heartbeat. "Fine, but Patterson is taking me. You can't drive worth a shit and almost killed me last time."

Higs rolled her eyes and helped Charley up off the floor. They walked slowly to the Jeep and Charley climbed into the passenger side.

"Do you even know how to drive, Patterson?" Charley asked.

"Yes ma'am."

Charley handed her the keys. "If you wreck us you're demoted to private."

"Yes, ma'am," Patterson smiled and started the Jeep.

After a short hair-raising ride over to Chico, they arrived at the hospital. Charley walked inside and was shown to a bed immediately. Patterson parked the Jeep and waited in the lobby.

Charley was laying back on the thin gurney when the curtain opened. She heard a loud gasp and opened her eyes.

"Audrey?" she said, blinking her eyes.

"Oh, Charley." Audrey ran across the short space, threw her arms around her, and kissed her soft cheek. "Oh how I've missed you."

"When did you get here?" Charley asked.

"This morning. I was sent straight to the hospital when I arrived. I haven't even checked into the nurses barracks. I'm sorry I didn't tell you, but by the time I found out it was too late to write." Audrey looked down at the woman in her arms and noticed the blood running down her forehead and across her cheek. "Oh my goodness, what have you done this time?" she said, pushing Charley's hair back to see the cut.

"Higs dropped a wing panel on my head," Charley said.

"This is a nasty cut."

"Can you stitch it up?"

"Yes," Audrey said, letting go of her long enough to grab the suture kit. "We have to stop meeting like this," she said when she started cleaning the cut.

Charley smiled. She thought she'd hit her head too hard or died when Audrey walked into the room. She couldn't remember the last time she'd seen a more beautiful sight. She closed her eyes and concentrated on the tenderness of Audrey's hands as she delicately closed the wound.

"You're all done," Audrey said, kissing her cheek.

"Will I get to see you tonight?" Charley asked.

"Do you want to see me tonight?" Audrey teased.

"I want to do more than see you," Charley whispered.

Audrey smiled and her cheeks colored.

"My shift ends in a few hours."

"Go ahead and get settled into the nurses' quarters. I'll come get you after dark," Charley said.

"Okay, and Major, try not to bump your head anymore. I'm quite fond of you and I'm afraid sewing your cuts isn't very romantic."

Charley laughed and shook her head.

"Oh hey, did Fran get sent here too?"

"Yes, she's still dealing with that broken arm so she's working the reception desk. She must have been getting supplies or something when you came in otherwise you would've seen her."

"I'll bring Higs with me tonight. Don't say anything to her."

Charley walked back out to the lobby and shooed Patterson out the door before Fran returned to the desk.

"You seem much better," Patterson said.

"Eight stitches will do that to a person."

***

"Since when do you want to go out? You haven't been off base in two months except for meetings. You've been a huge stick in the mud lately. That bump on your head must be worse than I thought," Higs said.

"Oh just get dressed and lets go," Charley huffed.

"Fine. Give me twenty minutes."

"Twenty minutes? I didn't say primp and put on a skirt for crying out loud. Just change your damn clothes!"

"Alright, alright. Don't get your knickers in a twist!"

"I don't wear knickers!" Charley stormed off towards her room to change into her WAAC Dress Uniform.

Five minutes later, Charley was beating on Higs' door. "Let's go!"

"Okay, good grief!" Higs followed her down the hallway and into the Jeep.

Charley kept quiet on the short drive over to Chico. When they entered the gates of the base, Higs began asking questions.

"Just wait a minute," Charley said, parking the Jeep by a group of white buildings. She cut the engine off and folded her hands over the steering wheel.

"How hard did you hit your head today?" Higs asked.

"Hard enough to know not to be late," Audrey said.

Higs screamed and jumped out of her seat. She spun around with her hand on her chest, gasping when she saw Audrey and Fran standing next to the Jeep laughing.

"Oh my God!" Higs said, jumping out and hugging both of them. "When did you get here?"

"Let them get in, Higs, so we can get the hell out of here," Charley shook her head and started the Jeep.

They drove to a small dive bar with a dance floor on the other side of town that was playing upbeat jive music and happy to serve anyone in uniform.

"How did you find this place?" Audrey asked when they sat down at a small round table on the edge of the tattered dance floor. The walls were in serious need of paint and the stools at the bar had springs showing where the cushion once was.

"When we first got here I took a drive and wandered into this place. The owner is a 'sister' although I don't think she's even admitted it to herself. Gladys said she rents rooms for the evening to soldiers that need a night away from the base," Charley said, ordering a round for their table when the waitress walked by.

"How does Gladys know about this place?" Higs asked.

"I didn't ask." Charley grinned.

"Who's Gladys?" Audrey asked.

"One of the ferry pilots and a 'sister'. She's almost as good at poker as the Major here."

"Did you say she rents rooms?" Fran asked.

Charley smiled and nodded.

"So, how did you know these two were here?" Higs asked, completely missing the conversation.

"It all started when you tried to kill me this afternoon," Charley said.

"Oh come on, it was an accident. I feel bad enough as it is. How was I to know that damn clamp would break?"

Charley shrugged. "Anyway, Audrey shocked the hell out of me when she appeared behind the curtain. I thought for sure I'd died and the first thing I was going to do was haunting you for the rest of your life." Charley laughed and took a sip of the whiskey the waitress set in front of her. "I realized she was real when she touched me and then I was so happy you'd hit me with that wing I could've kissed your ass."

"We got our orders and literally flew out less than twenty-four hours later. There was no way to write and neither of us had any idea how to get a phone call to either of you. When we arrived this morning the CO immediately put us on duty. It was just fate I guess that Charley came into the hospital."

"Yeah, fate. That's what I call it too," Charley glared at Higs and grinned.

"How's your head?" Fran asked.

"It's fine. How are you?" Charley said, looking at the cast on her arm.

"Better now," Fran said, patting Higs' hand and squeezing.

Charley was about to ask Audrey if she wanted to dance when a round woman with thick gray hair walked up to their table. She cleared her scratchy throat and bent down.

"Will you ladies be requiring rooms for the evening?"

Charley looked at the table then back at the woman.

"Two rooms please," she said.

When the woman walked away, Audrey grabbed Charley's leg under the table causing her to jerk and smack her knee on the table top.

"Did I just miss something?" Higs asked.

"You can thank me in the morning," Charley said as the woman returned with two keys.

***

Charley unbuttoned her jacket and laid it over the back of the small chair in the corner of the room. Audrey kicked off her shoes and sat on the edge of the small bed.

"I've missed you so much," Audrey said.

"I've missed you too. I don't ever want to go through the hell of knowing something happened to you but not knowing whether or not you are alive. It damn near drove me crazy," Charley said, sitting down next to her.

"I'm not leaving again. Fran and I both asked to stay at Chico for the rest of our service and we only have about a year left anyway. I don't care to ever see the frontlines of this war again."

Charley wrapped her arms around Audrey, pulled her close, and kissed her lips softly.

"Falling in love with you has been the best thing that has ever happened to me," Charley said.

"Loving you kept me alive when that ship was sinking. I kept thinking if something happens to me

Charley will never know. I just knew somehow I had to get off that boat and get to you." She ran her hand over Charley's cheek and kissed her.

"I know I have close to two more years and initially I'd planned to re-sign for another two at least, but that little house on the edge of the river is sounding better and better every day," Charley said. "So, if you'll have me, I'm going to ask to finish up my service here at Chico and then spend the rest of my life making you happy."

"Charley, there is nothing more in this world that I want than to spend the rest of my life looking at your smiling face."

About the Author

Graysen Morgen was born and raised in North Florida with winding rivers and waterways at her back door and the white sandy beach a mile away. She has spent most of her lifetime in the sun and on the water. She enjoys reading, writing, fishing, and spending as much time as possible with her partner and their daughter.

You can contact Graysen at graysenmorgen@aol.com and like her fan page on facebook.com/graysenmorgen